LEGACY

LEGACY

In Search of the Past

KATHY G. WIDENER

Deeds Publishing | Athens

Published by Deeds Publishing in Athens, GA
www.deedspublishing.com

Printed in The United States of America

Cover and interior design by Deeds Publishing

Photo by Adam Kring on Unsplash

ISBN 978-1-961505-12-4

Books are available in quantity for promotional or premium use. For information, email info@deedspublishing.com.

First Edition, 2023

10 9 8 7 6 5 4 3 2 1

This Book is dedicated to my Daddy, Robert Kelly Gantt. He was always a good friend and a great storyteller. He was a dependable father, calm, and gentle like his mother, Florence. He never cursed, not even if a situation warranted strong language. He took my siblings and me to church on Sundays, even after my mother disappeared from our childhood. I always knew I was loved, even though he didn't say so until he got old and infirm. Then he would hug me and tell me he loved me before I went out the door. He was born November 6, 1923, and passed from this earth on a Sunday morning February 22, 2015. If he was still with us, he would be one hundred years old.

"When people look inside
my life, I want to hear
them say
She's got her father's eyes
Her father's eyes
Eyes that find the good in
things
When good is not around"
—Amy Grant

Contents

Preface

Genealogy began to become an important part of my life in childhood, long before the internet and social media were available to humanity.

I had been thoroughly schooled in the art of storytelling from my early childhood. I remember distinctly sitting on the front porch at the old wooden clapboard house I grew up in. Most times, I would sit quietly and listen to the stories of my ancestors the older generation talked about. A lot of their descriptions I could not comprehend, relationships from a hundred years before were of no concern to an eight-year-old child. But their stories about moonshine stills, the producing of the fiery liquid, the effect its consumption had on friends and kinfolks; of course, their stories of evading the law were too mind boggling to ignore.

The front porch, in the Spring and early Fall was just a comforting place to be. The lights were off, and the only light came through the screen doors of the hallway and of course the night sky with a million bright pinpricks of light on a blanket of black. The moon when it rose above the horizon, was a brilliant orb that shone through the dense woods of scrub oaks across the road. I would listen awhile, then become distracted by the lightening bugs darting about across the dirt road and in the edges of the yard and the calls of night birds, owls, and whippoorwills. It was always quiet, no traffic, lots of laughter. The memories from those nights I cherish and relive them in my thoughts many nights as I nod off to sleep.

My siblings and I witnessed the grown ups' stories many nights after supper on that front porch. We would listen a while then as restless, bored children tend to do, then play a familiar game, 'you're it', a game of chase, or our favorite, 'booger man', marching up and down the brick lined walk singing "Ain't no booger man out tonight cause daddy killed them all." Of course we knew one of the siblings was hiding out by the road to scare us. They would jump out from behind the bushes, or the big dirt filled wash tubs on either side, that held our grandma's elephant ears screaming "boooo" and waving their hands above their heads. Sometimes, it was the stealth approach, crawling out and blocking our path with a loud growl. When they did, we would run screaming to the porch, even though we were expecting it. Not one of the grownups admonished our screaming, even though we interrupted one of their stories.

The porch always had a laid-back atmosphere. If we were not arguing among ourselves, the grownups had the ability to ignore our laughter and chatter. They let kids be kids.

As I grew older, I began to understand these were their

memories and someday they would not be here to tell us their stories. I began to really want to know more about my family. I started researching my Gantt family, going to cemeteries, archives, and talking to older family members. I have a multitude of notes, documents, maps, and family stories.

I grew up, finished high school, married the love of my life, and raised three beautiful children. I was for many years a stay-at-home mom. After my children were all in school, I had more time to research my genealogy. I joined the Lexington County Genealogy Society, read lots of books, joined societies dependent on ancestry, and went back to college eighteen years after graduating from high school. My main interests were literature and history, of course.

I inherited lots of old family pictures and have preserved them in scrapbooks and eventually published four books. My books are all about memories, with pictures included. After I published my fourth book, _Every Life Tells a Story_, in 2021, I thought my writing days were over. After all, I had covered the lives of my great grandparents, my grandparents, parents, my siblings, and myself growing up, what more could I possibly need to write about.

I was a member of a local Writers Group in Aiken County; they were a big help in many ways, and I appreciate all their input. One of my writing friends suggested I write a prequel. I have thought long and hard about this idea and prayed for guidance. I have decided to give it a shot. I certainly have the documents and information. I knew all about my immigrant ancestor, Peter Gaunt, where he lived, and his family.

I am now a member of a British Ancestry Group online through Facebook. I wrote a post about my immigrant ancestor, Peter Gaunt and where he may have lived in England. Someone in answer to my post stated that Gaunt was a Norman name. A light came on in my brain, I had taken a British History class in college in 1990. I wrote an extensive account entitled "William the Conqueror and The Battle of Hastings". Of course, I still have the complete document with all documentation. Genealogists, at least in my family, tend to keep everything. I thought my findings would make a wonderful prologue to the prequel.

Humorous Genealogy Quote, Moment of Truth for a genealogist: discovering you are your own cousin.

"This is really truth; I am my own
cousin and can prove it."

May 20, 2023

Prologue:
William the Conqueror and the Battle of Hastings:

Synopsis of the Invasion

The year was 1066, the crown of England was the prize. William, Duke of Normandy challenged King Harold of England on the plains of Hastings, on England's southern coast. That autumn day, October 14, 1066, the most decisive battle in England's history raged. Its outcome determined the course of a nation.

William was born at Falaise, Normandy, in 1027, the son of Robert the 1st, Duke of Normandy, and Herleve, a tanner's daughter. In 1034, Robert the 1st departed on a crusade to the holy land. Before leaving, he brought forth his young son as his heir. In 1035, upon the death of his father, William became the Duke of Normandy.

There were many who wanted to challenge his legitimate right, "Walter, the brother of Herleve, was wont at this time to sleep in the company of his nephew, Duke William, and frequently at night was forced to fly for safety with his charge to take refuge in the cottages of the poor" (Douglas 40). He had to fight for survival and fighting became his way of life.

Edward the Confessor had suggested the prospect of the English crown to William and upon Edward's death, William expected the English throne would be his. William's Aunt Emma had been married to King Ethelred. Emma and King Ethelred were Edward's parents, making Edward and Duke William first cousins. At Edward's death in January 1066, Earl Harold Godwinson was declared King by the Witan, wise men who were the King's Counsel in Anglo-Saxon, England. When news of the usurper's ascension reached William in Normandy, he was determined to seize the throne of England for himself and to destroy Harold.

William began to organize his army and prepare for an invasion. "To the power of Normandy would be added the strength of many allies drawn from all of Europe by the Justice of his cause and the promise of rich rewards" (Butler 62). Pope Alexander even championed Duke William's cause, allowing his ships to sail under the papal banner, even though he would send no soldiers. "A War founded on greed and wounded vanity became a crusade" (Butler 80). The ships built to move the Duke's army would wait on Normandy's coast for a southerly wind, but the weather did not cooperate.

In early September the weather changed and preparations to embark began. Supplies, machines of war, horses, and men hurried aboard the waiting ships. September 28, 1066, Williams's fleet landed at Pevensey and marched overland to the port of Hastings. He had landed in England unchallenged and would remain at Hastings for fear of being trapped inland.

Duke William's Norman army numbered perhaps, 8,000 soldiers, 3,000 horsemen, one thousand archers, and the rest in infantry. The English army had no cavalry and archers. This fact became the deciding factor. "The Battle of Hastings has been described as a victory over infantry won by cavalry supported by the long-range weapon of the archers" (Douglas 202).

The bloody battle begins on the morning of October 14, 1066. Lasting until nightfall, it turned into unspeakable slaughter. The great English army had been defeated, Harold killed, and William discarded the name of Duke, and assumed the royal title.

King William was strong-willed and ruled his subjects with an iron hand. That iron hand was also tempered with justice. "No one however powerful dared do anything against his will, and as a result any honest man could travel over his kingdom without injury with his bosom full of gold, and no man dared strike or kill another" (Douglas 373).

There is no doubt this one man and his victory at the Battle of Hastings made a great impression on the future history of England and indeed the world.

Eyewitness To the Norman Invasion

By: Kathy Gantt Widener
November 21,1990
British History 311

Of the eight thousand plus warriors that accompanied Duke William of Normandy, only about fifty can be identified definitely. Gilbert of Ghent, son of Count Baldwin of Flanders and the nephew of Duke William, was one of those fifty. Upon the death of Eleanor May Gant in 1924, a journal belonging to Gilbert was discovered at Moyne House, Essex, England. Along with Gilbert's journal, a document showing the house and estate as a possession of Miss Gant's ancestors since the conquest was also discovered. Gilbert's journal dated 1066 details his thoughts and experiences during the invasion of England and his part in the Battle of Hastings. The following is a transcription of entries from Gilbert's journal:

20 January 1066 — Ghent

A courier arrived at court today with news of the death of King Edward of England. The throne has been seized by Earl Harold. I fear this news brings only trouble to all Flanders. Duke William will seek revenge. We wait upon his messenger that is sure to come soon.

16 February 1066 — Ghent

A messenger from Duke William arrived today. The duke wishes my father to attend a special council at Rouen within a fortnight. It can only mean he is determined to fight for what was promised him, the throne of England. I will accompany my father, along with twenty of our knights.

23 February 1066 — Rouen

The great and small wait upon the Duke's word. My father, Baldwin of Flanders, joins Eustace of Boulogne, Ponthieu, and Brittany at the Duke's request. Also present are Normans considered of some statue.

Robert the Crafty and his kindred from Italy have been summoned. There is also rumor that Gilbert of Lisieux has been sent to Rome, we may cry a holy war and call on Christendom to defeat Harold.

It is cold in Rouen and all present wish only for hearth and home. But Harold has broken his promise, and all the Duke's allies and kinsmen will stand with him. He is not an easy man to defy, even if the heart speaks otherwise. Duke William is fair to his own but woe unto all who are against him. When he speaks before the council, all will listen. He has a voice like thunder and dark piercing eyes that command obedience.

I accompanied the Duke on a stag hunt last winter and marveled at his strength and bravery. We were accompanied by two bowmen when a wild boar attacked from a stand of firs. The Duke calmly stood his ground. He had not time to fix an arrow in his bow but stood ready with a spear to meet the animal's charge. The Duke threw the spear, which pierced the animal's heart and the animal dropped not three feet from where William stood.

I am indeed proud that the Duke is my kinsman. Duchess Matilda is my father's own sister. There will be no recourse but for father to agree to whatever Duke William wants. We must stand by our kinsman when his honor has been challenged.

2 March 1066 — Rouen

Duke William's messengers from England returned to him and were brought before him in the armory of his castle at Rouen. He had demanded that Earl Harold relinquish the throne as promised. The messenger was treated well by Earl Harold, but the reply was not what the Duke wanted to hear. According to the Knight of Bayeux that delivered the message, Harold bade William to come. He would not need to seek for him in corners. I fear the worst is now necessary. The Duke is determined.

4 March 1066 — Rouen

The Duke requested my presence along with fathers at a meeting of the council. The Duke laid his case before his allies and Barons, leaving no room for dissent. Edward the Confessor had dangled the prospect of the throne before William in 1051 upon Williams's visit to England. He possesses royal blood and is related to the late king. Another reason cited by William is the oath Earl Harold Godwinson swore to him at this very court in 1052.

The Duke considered Earl Harold his friend and had knighted him in the Norman fashion. Earl Harold has seized the throne that is rightfully the Duke's, and he is determined to invade England and reclaim that right. A man's oath is a sacred thing and to break it is truly a dirty deed. Few men would have questioned the Duke's motives at the council meeting. It would have been more foolhardy than brave. I am afraid he does not take criticism or dissent in an easy manner. With his determination, all present chose the safest course, complete compliance.

20 March 1066 — Rouen

We start for home on the morrow to begin preparation for the invasion of England. Father has promised twenty-five ships and one thousand knights to William's service. I am to lead our knights and to have a ship under my command. The Duke has asked my service as one of his lieutenants and I am indeed honored.

A most strange occurrence I will record here. Last evening while the Duke sat at the evening meal, some servants rushed shouting into the hall. They had seen a great star in the heavens, and all were terribly afraid it was a bad omen. The Duke just laughed and said, "Ye are simple

men, why do you stand there quaking it is a sign of terror."
I witnessed the star myself and it was indeed frightful to
behold. It was brilliantly bright with a long tail that spread
across the heavens. All who witnessed Duke William's
words concerning the star have spread the news. It is indeed the sword of God drawn against Harold. The terror
of servants has turned to rejoicing. All believe now it is a
good sign.

1 April 1066 — Ghent

All is in readiness for our departure to the lower valley of
the Dives on Normandy's coast. There our shipbuilders
will build the vessels that will carry our knights across the
channel to England. I will be absent from home at least
until next spring. I dread the prospect of winter in England
but am honored to be part of the Duke's great plan. It is
so hard to bid farewell to father and mother and all I hold
dear. God grant our mission success. It is a worthy course
we steer and all that is needed is His divine guidance.

6 June 1066 — Normandy coast

It is done. Our ships have been built and we only wait for
the Duke's command. The weather is fine, and the wind
often blows from the south and the southwest. Men mur-
mur at the delay, but they are well fed and are kept hard at
work. Most are content to wait and trust their fortune to

Duke William. The Duke has spies that constantly cross the channel to bring word from England. Harold's army waits for us, but the Duke seems unconcerned. His spies say Harold's army is low on food and there is some dissension among the English Barons. The Duke feels Harold must disband his army ere long and that we must keep patience.

15 June 1066 — Normandy coast

Gilbert of Lisieux arrived today with word from Rome. The pope supports the Duke's case against Harold's deceit. The papal banner will fly above our army as a sign this is indeed a holy mission.

1 July 1066

Harold's fleet still keeps the seas and England's shores are still guarded from west to east, garrisoned like a fortress. Bishop Odo says we cannot be much longer. There have even been whispers among the men that the Duke is afraid. He of course does not hear these whispers. All are afraid of him. Even the countryside round about this great camp has no fear from marauders. The Duke doles out justice and expects his men to be honorable when dealing with his countrymen. There are certainly some devious scoundrels in this army encampment; mercenaries that are only here because of the prospect of plundering England's countryside. As long as they fight when the time comes, the Duke will not question their conduct in England. Until then they fear a wrong move could mean their lives. All are on their best behavior.

5 July 1066 — Normandy coast

Spies from England say Harold's army is restless. There are many desertions. Few folk believe the Duke will come and the harvest calls them home. This is good news for us. If we stay in Normandy much longer, he is sure to disband and recall his fleet.

13 August 1066 — Normandy coast

Duke Williams's fleet fills the river Dives, lying side to side so close that a man might cross the river, as by bridge. Upon the hills above, the knights and warriors are encamped, and their tents spread for miles. Before the tents of the Barons their standards flutter in the breeze. The rains that plagued our camp for three weeks have abated but the wind does not cooperate with our plan. My servant sees to my every need but I long to begin the invasion and finish our mission. Those around me feel the same way. All are restless. The Duke most of all. He paces back and forth in front of his pavilion.

Three foreign knights have requested permission to withdraw from our enterprise. The Duke granted their release saying such men do best by the fireside and that warriors of Normandy drive a bolder bargain. Normans would not be satisfied with a month's wage when all the gold in England waited for them. The Normans mocked the knights, and they departed in shame. William's men have a renewed determination to see the invasion to its conclusion.

8 September 1066 — Normandy coast

Each day masses are sung, and prayers offered for a fair wind. Nonetheless, the weather remains cold and wild, and the wind blows from the north. All are discouraged. Our prayers and offerings seem to be to no avail. We must give more. The Saints are hard to win. The Duke spoke to his men and announced a day of fast and prayer on the morrow. When he spoke to them one of the soldiers spat and he was beaten for it. If all else fails, then shall St. Valeri's bones be borne through all the camp.

10 September 1066 — Normandy coast

The wind has changed. Preparation to disembark has begun. The camp is in an uproar. Supplies, machines of war, horses, and weapons are being made ready. My servant polished my armor and my weapons. We all await the Duke's signal, but preparations are hurried. There is much to do when moving an army of eight thousand men. The ships must be loaded with all our equipment. It will be necessary to take an abundant supply of food, we will forage and live off the land once we have landed in England.

Spies brought word to the Duke that Harold's army has disbanded, and his fleet returned to the Thames. That is hard to believe, and we must be cautious and expect the worse.

26 September 1066 — Normandy coast

Finally, the day has arrived. All is in readiness. We set sail at dawn tomorrow for England. My standard has been transferred to my ship and I will sleep there tonight. Forty of my best knights will accompany me along with my personal servant. By the Duke's order, the soldiers will be armed and ready before the English coast is reached. Even though reports place Harold's army elsewhere, we must be prepared.

28 September 1066 — Hastings peninsula

Our fleet landed at Pevensey and marched overland to Hastings. Hastings is on a peninsula and will offer good defense. There is no sign of Harold's army, but the Duke has made no decision as to our next move. We have been ordered to stay close to the coast and the soldiers are digging entrenchments and building temporary fortifications.

We have landed unchallenged, but staying at Hastings is dangerous, we could be trapped here.

3 October 1066 — Hastings peninsula

Supplies are running low, and we must make a move. Duke William sees our best hope in provoking an early attack. To do this he has ordered the countryside near Hastings pillaged for provisions and goods. Killing and burning is sure to force the English dogs to make a move. We cannot afford to delay.

5 October 1066 — Hastings peninsula

Word has reached our camp that King Harold's army has defeated the Norsemen in York to the North. The Duke called a counsel to discuss what we should do. Some believe we should press on to London and take the city. Duke William said we will lie and wait for further favorable tidings. The men must forage on all sides and bring in corn and cattle.

7 October 1066 — Hastings peninsula

An Englishman, sent by Robert Wymarcson, the Essex Sheriff, brought a message to the Duke. Robert is a kinsman to William and only counsels for his good. The Englishman said the King is on the road to London at full speed. The Housecarles with him. The whole strength of Mercia and Northumbria is following. The fyrd of Wessex and East Anglia are gathering in the city. The fleet makes ready. He believes we should flee. Duke William replies he will return when he has what he came to seek.

We must not be frightened by these English dogs; we will yet have victory. Instead of cowering at the message, the Duke sends a message of his own. He has bid all his captains to range more widely, slay all that lives, and destroy and burn. Let the land run with blood. Fire and destruction will be a spur to Harold's army. They will come soon.

12 October 1066 — Hastings peninsula

King Harold's army is nearby. Last night I could see their campfires in the distance. Messengers are sent back and fore between the camps, but no agreement can be reached. Harold must pay for his treachery and the Duke will not except less than the throne. The only recourse is battle.

14 October 1066 — Hastings peninsula

Battle begins at about 9:00 this morning. I write this amid the carnage that remains. I, myself, feel lucky to have survived, so many fell this day. Harold's army has been destroyed and the Duke has the victory. The battle went like this. The main force of the English was stationed on Senlac Ridge, a rise some 275 feet high and sealed off on either side by rapidly falling ground. At first the Duke used his archers, but the shield wall of the English diverted the arrows. William then sent his mounted men hoping to give them opportunity to use their swords. I led my father's knights up the hill on horseback. The English broke rank and met us halfway. I slashed with my sword, splitting the head of one Englishman, and chopping off another's arm. The field was littered with dead and dying and blood covered everything. I received a slight wound to my shoulder, but the main thrust was diverted by quick action. It seems that during this time the Duke ordered the archers to fire over the heads of the Englishmen and an arrow struck King Harold in the eye. Battle turned into slaughter and the Englishmen were destroyed. The battle was won, but at a terrible cost in lives. It was a day of horror that I can never forget. England will be William's now. There is no one strong enough to resist the Duke and our army. Tomorrow, we bury our dead and march inland toward London. The Duke is weary and refuses to speak to anyone. He is spending this night amid the carnage on Senlac Ridge. Two hundred fifteen of my father's knights were killed and seventy-nine wounded. The wounded will survive but must remain behind while the rest of the army marches inland. The great English army has been defeated. Harold is dead and now William will discard the name of duke and assume the royal title.

25 December 1066 — Canterbury Cathedral

Today in Canterbury Cathedral, Duke William was crowned as England's King. The conquest was a success, and I was honored to serve my lord. With spring I will leave this cursed country and return to my homeland, Flanders. I may within the year return to claim the lands the Duke awarded to me for my service to him. He has indeed been very generous and since my older brother inherits father's title, I may yet seek my fortune here.

Gilbert of Ghent was well rewarded for his participation in the conquest and his loyalty to his uncle, Duke William. He had the lands of one Tour, a Dane, given him. Also given to him were lands in Berkshire, Oxfordshire, Yorkshire, Cambridgeshire, Buckinghamshire, Huningdon, Northton, Essex, Rutland, and Warwickshire. He also received lordships in the county of Lincoln of which Folkingham, he made his principal seat, and head of his barony. He married Alice, daughter and heir of Hugh de Montfort, a great baron of that age. Eventually the family name became Gant and Miss Eleanor May Gant, in whose home the journal was discovered, was a direct descendant of Gilbert's.

This eyewitness account was part of my British history assignment. A slice of life, my professor called it. I was to put myself in a particular year in British history, use the vernacular to the time and circumstance as if I lived in that time and place. I chose the Norman invasion and Gilbert de Ghent as my eyewitness because, true to my Gantt family research, I am a descendant of Gilbert. According to Burke's, "Extinct Peerage" in the eleventh century, the de Gant, or Gaunts of England, according to all heraldic records, came to England with the Norman Legions and participated in the triumph of the Battle of Hastings. Historically the eyewitness account is true, but actually I concocted the whole journal business.

There was a Miss Eleanor May Gant who died at the age of 88 at Moyne House, Essex, England, 1921. With her death, a continuous holding of over 900 years was brought to a close. A document still in existence shows that the house and estate were a possession of Miss Gant's ancestors before the conquest (1066), and a portion of the present building dates back to the time of Edward the 3rd (1327-1377). Evidently Miss Eleanor had no children.

The above taught me two lessons. 1) I have too much information about my ancestors and 2) It is so true; you can't take it with you!

Kathy G. Widener

Gaunt Coat of Arms

Introduction

The author represents the 12th generation since the Gaunts left England. The 1st generation researched is Thomas Gaunt born the 7th of July 1571 in England and his second wife Susanne Bates Gaunt. Thomas was a tanner in Lincolnshire, England; this book will examine each successive generation since. I have constructed a timeline, and every generation will be examined towards present day; names, dates, way of life, and particulars about the where and when they lived, also stories about each generation that I have available.

I have been researching my Gantt/Gauntt family since the mid 1970's, spending hours speaking to family members, collecting their stories. I have found some fascinating anecdotes to share with my readers. I began this research journey fifty years ago, most of the early interviews were conducted with family members who are no longer with us. I will give dates of each generation through my direct line, but will add the names of all siblings, and information and stories about them where available.

My Gaunt family emigrant ancestor was Peter Gaunt who arrived in Plymouth Colony, Massachusetts in the year 1636. Peter and others converted to the Quaker belief newly introduced in Sandwich. In 1653, the Quakers began to be persecuted by the Puritans, the Quakers were harassed and fined, including Peter Gaunt. The Gaunts migrated, first to Rhode Island then to West Jersey. Hananiah, son of Peter, moved to Burlington County, West Jersey in 1685 where he purchased land. After Hananiah's death son, Zebulon Gaunt Sr. remained on the farm left to him in his father's will, raised his family, and is believed to be buried on the property. Four of Zebulon's children left West Jersey in 1743, this can be verified by letters written to their NJ relatives.

The four siblings, Zebulon 2nd, Sophie Gaunt Mathis, Dorothy Gaunt Teague, and Israel Gaunt headed south, first to North Carolina New Garden Monthly Meeting in Orange County, North Carolina, then Camden, SC where Sophie Gantt Mathis died in 1761, then Israel Gaunt migrated a little further south to Newberry, SC. Israel Gaunt was my direct ancestor and I joined the DAR as his descendant. Finally, one of his sons, Joseph Gauntt arrived in Lexington County, SC.

This book, like my four previously published books will be written as a narrative, based on real people and their real stories. But this is a prequel to all the others and most probably will be my last published work. I promise to try to make it the best.

1. Thomas Gaunt — England

Thomas Gaunt was born on the 22nd of July 1571 in Silkstone Parish, Yorkshire, England. He lived there most of his life and supported his family as a tanner. Being a tanner of animal hides to produce leather was not an easy job or a clean one. It would most certainly qualify for Mike Rowe's present day 'Dirty Jobs' and 'Somebody's Got To Do It'. Tanning of animal hides was situated at the outside edge of the town because it produced an odorous smell, and it took place near a river or stream.

Thanks to the internet, I learned way more than I needed to know about the 16th century job of tanners. First, the hides were soaked and softened in a lime pit to burn off the animal hair and flesh debris. Next step, the skins were washed with chicken droppings diluted in water. Hence the location near a river or stream. After the skins were washed, any remaining hair had to be scraped off manually by the tanner with scrapping tools. Finally, the hides spent a few months soaking in the tannin basins. The tannin powder came from the ground bark of trees mixed with water. The tanner was the middleman that stood between hunters and the butchers that provided him with hides. It was definitely a dirty occupation, but leather was in great demand for shoes, harnesses, and saddles. Thomas knew he had to feed and clothe his wife and children, and somebody had to do it.

According to the Parish registry found in Lincoln, England evidently Thomas had at least two wives. He married Susanne Bates the 28th of August 1609 in Rotherham, Yorkshire and moved to Lincoln, a town located in the east midlands region of England about 156 miles north of London. Evidently, they moved fairly soon after their marriage. Their son, Peter, was baptized 29th of June 1610 at St. Peters at Gowts in Lincoln, England, their parish church. Thomas had an older son, George, for whom he left most of his York lands and a daughter, both mentioned in his will.

People relied on their fellow townsmen to defend their reputation and to protect each other, watch their back in modern day speak. Leaving your hometown was not something you do without considerable preparation or in a state of desperation. So why did Susanne and Thomas leave Yorkshire? That is a question we can never answer. According to my records, there are several Bates men living in Lincoln, maybe the move was instigated by Susanne because, they were her relations.

When Thomas and Susanne lived in Lincoln, the population of Lincoln was fewer than 5,000, London's population was 200,000. Much of the countryside was used for grazing. Sheep were most prevalent; they could provide wool for clothing and food. Cattle, a much larger animal, could be used for food and their hides produced leather. During this time period, because of improvements in husbandry, the care and cultivation of crops and animals, villages, and towns were growing into large cities.

At this time in England the medium age of the population was 22 years. If a citizen lived past the age of 60 years, they were considered lucky indeed. The over sixty population in England was only 7.3%. Thomas lived to age 55, which was considered old age.

The social order of Thomas and Susanne's day totally centered around the four levels: gentleman, prosperous townsmen, country men, and craftsmen. Married women had no rights, their husband was considered the head of the family. They, however, were in charge of their household, so marriage did have an advantage for women. Unmarried females that lived with a father and mother, their father was in charge. At least being a wife added the management of the household, directing the work of any servants, and controlling purchases for their family. Single women could have no profession. They may travel, pray, write, and go about freely as a man. So, I say, it was our modern day saying, six of one or half a dozen of the other.

The really sad social level was the poor. They lived in run down abandoned tenements, basically as squatters, or on the street in towns, sleeping on a bed of straw beside the roadway, no food except for begging or stealing to survive. Most of the itinerant poor were young boys. I immediately thought of Charles Dickens and Oliver Twist, the story of a young boy, with no family, begging and stealing to survive. A sad gang of miscreants working for a despicable leader named Fagin on the streets of London.

I believe the best way to understand the lives of my ninth great grandparents, Thomas and Susanne Bates Gaunt of England, is in their own words. I have the transcriptions of both their wills, Thomas died 1621 in Lincoln, England, Susanne Bates Gaunt died in 1626.

The following are their own words from their transcribed wills:

Thomas Gaunt will dated 12 July 1621 …

Susanne, widow of Thomas Gaunt of St. Peter at Gowts, County and city of Lincoln, England, and Thomas Bates (her brother) helped with the inventory of his property at his death; women could not resolve legal matters by themselves, thus Thomas Gaunt names Thomas Bates to help. Each room in their home was listed and then a value placed on each item after the inventory by Susanne and Thomas Bates was verified by three other men, before the value was excepted. I found this fascinating, the different rooms themselves and their contents.

In the Parlor: this includes dishes, pewter, blankets, canopy bedstead, his purse and apparel (the deceased Thomas Gaunt), pair of sheets, blankets trundle bed, linen cupboard, two candle sticks, a broom, a chamber pot, two tables, six buffet stools, one creamer, and six saucers. It appears to me this was a large room, probably with a fireplace for receiving guests, but there was also a bed. Since Thomas Gaunt's apparel and purse were included in this room, he might have slept here near the fireplace for warmth in cold weather.

In the Hall: one long table, one square table, two carpets, six cushions, two chairs, candlesticks. This could have served as a summer parlor for entertaining visitors.

In the bed chamber: one truss bed (bed with a wooden frame with ropes to support the mattress), one rug, two blankets, two coverlets, another bed, two dozen and a half napkin, two towels, and seven barst (a coarse fabric), one chest, one desk, and one cupboard and a bolster (a long pillow placed under other pillows for support). This appears to be the primary bedroom, where they bathed due to the mention of towels and napkins (perhaps modern-day washcloths) They would have used ewers (large jugs with a wide mouth) to carry water and a shallow bowl to pour the water in.

In the kitchen: 3 brass pots, one kettle, seven pans, two skillets, one chafing dish, two spits, one land iron (what we called fire dogs, pieces of iron rod with feet in the front and back to hold wood in the fireplace) one dripping pan and a gallow tree (to hold meat above the fire). I was surprised there was a kitchen inside the dwelling. In the early years in America, there was a separate kitchen house to cook in because of the danger of fire.

There was also a brew house and a list of the animals the Gaunts owned.

In the yard: two cattle, two heifers, two calves, two colts, seventeen sheep, two stocks of bees (for their honey), and implements for the tanning trade. Total value of inventory 62 lbs. 16 shillings 8 pence

According to the conversion chart for English currency in the year 1621, Thomas Gaunt was a skilled tradesman and the inventory amount would be his wages for 1256 days. This information comes from the National Archives in the form of a currency converter. I would say Thomas and Suzanne were considered well to do at that time period.

To me, the inventory of my ancestor's home was fascinating and gave insight into their lives. I wonder if Thomas was raising his cattle, heifers, calves, and sheep for his tanning business, to butcher and turn their hides into leather, I'm sure that was not the case. As a young child I can remember the threat from my parents, "Do you want me to tan your hide?" Since researching my family, that threat takes on a new connotation.

The actual will of Thomas Gaunt was dated the 4th of April 1621. Evidently, he expected his demise would come soon. He was buried on the 14th of April 1621, only ten days after it was written or dictated in front of witnesses. There is no way to learn how ill he was or the cause of death. A few excerpts to follow:

I Thomas Gaunt of the parish of St. Peter at Gowts in Lincoln sick in body but of good and perfect memory, God be thanked. 1st I wholly commit and commend my soul to God which gave it to me, beseeching him to accept it with his mercy and heavenly blessing for his mercy sake in Jesus Christ, my alone Savior.

I will that Susanne, my 'now wife' shall peacefully have and enjoy the measure of my enclosures, lands, and tenements (not sold away) in the county of York in the parish of Silkstone. After her decease, my lands in York to my eldest son, George & his heirs. I also give "my now wife" furniture to the value of 10 lbs. and 10 lbs. lawful money as her share. After her decease to Peter Gaunt, my son, and his heirs. The rest of my goods and chattels I give and bequeath to James my son and Dynes and guardians for my only son, Anne, my daughters, to be given 20 lbs. each. Anne will receive her part when she reaches the full age of twenty and one.

What stands out in Thomas's will? To me, the fact he addresses Susanne as his 'now wife' speaks to the fact there was at least one other wife, possibly more. He mentions George, James, Dynis, and Anne as his other children. Peter, I know, is Susanne's son. In that time period, many women died in childbirth and Thomas had at least three sons, two mentioned in his will, the other Jacob, baptized in Lincoln the 27th of September 1596 may have died young, and two daughters. I have identified two other possible wives, Cecily Carter March 1600, and Isabelle Wheelwright (widow) 9 October 1602. The years of 1600 and 1602 may be when Thomas married them and again may not and who cares three hundred years after the fact. Reading Thomas's will, I noted he seemed to be a very religious man and was thankful for God's giving him his soul and for his long memory. He also left ten shillings to the poor of the parish where he dwelled, so if the records are correct, he must have been a good and decent man.

Susanne Bates Gaunt wrote or dictated her will on the 12th of February 1626. She was buried on the 25th of February 1626, only 13 days later. They both didn't have much time to get their affairs in order, could be procrastinators, maybe that is a Gantt personality trait, I tend to do the same. The first item in Susanne's will after declaring her faith in God was remembering the poor of the parish, but she was more generous than Thomas, she left 30 shillings of lawful English money. She also left 10 shillings each to her brothers Adam and Thomas. Most importantly Susanne said, "I do make and order Alexander Pell of the city of Lincoln, tanner and Robert Wood of the said city, dyer, supervisors of this my last will and testament and I do make and order them as protectors of Peter Gaunt, unto his lawful age of one and twenty years and I do give unto either of them for their pains ten shillings lawful English money. The condition of this obligation is such that whereas the Alexander Pell and Robert Wood are lawfully elected constitutionally, appointed confirmed tutors, guardians, and curators of Peter Gaunt." Peter was only sixteen when his mother died, he would be given an education which was very important, there were so many in England at this time that could not even write their name.

> "History is the witness that testifies to the
> passing of time; It illuminates reality, vitalizes
> memory, provides guidance in daily life,
> and brings us tidings of Ancient times."
>
> —Marcus Tullius Cicero

St. Peters at Gowts, Lincoln England

2.Peter Gaunt Coming to America

Peter Gaunt was my earliest ancestor to arrive in the new world. It was not the United States at that time, or even the thirteen original colonies, it was just hopefully a new world and a new beginning. Peter set sail with his wife, Lydia Hampton and at least two of their children, Peter and Lydia. The repetition of family first names would later make it extremely difficult to distinguish one generation from the next. At that time in history, it did not matter, and children were, of course, named after their father and mother or grandparents. As many of Peter and Lydia's fellow citizens, they left England to flee religious persecution and oppression in England by emigrating to Massachusetts Bay Colony. They were transported by the London Company from St. Bridget's Parish, London, to Scituate, Massachusetts. They were transported on a ship named The Mayflower, not the Mayflower of Plymouth Rock fame.

The original Mayflower was likely scrapped. It made only one other trip to the new world. The great significance of the original would not become important until it was too late. It was on the original that the Mayflower Compact was written and signed, the first document to establish self-government in the new world and the occupants that made friends with native Americans, leading to establishment of a National holiday on the last Thursday of November in 1777, Thanksgiving Day.

What was it like for the families on this tiny ship in a Big Ocean? The ship Peter and his family sailed on was barely over 100 feet in length and 24 feet wide. The crew consisted of cooks, sailors, carpenters, officers, and a surgeon to see to the ills of those on board. The crew numbered 37 souls. They lived in small cabins above the main deck. All passengers and their families were relegated to an area between the main deck and the cargo hole which covered the bottom level of the ship. The cargo hole was the storage for all food supplies, fresh water, and ballast of bricks to help stabilize the ship.

Quarters for the miserable 101 passengers was a bare windowless area 60 by 24 feet. The plank floor and the low ceiling of five feet was so confining, in nice weather those that were physically able would climb the wooden ladder to the main deck just to be able to stand and move around in the fresh air. Fresh water was scarce and could not be wasted on bathing, it was only for drinking. Most of the passengers drink beer as a beverage, the fresh water was so precious. Fresh food, vegetables and smoked meats were used quickly. Three weeks into the voyage, the only nourishment for the cramped travelers consisted of salted pork, dried fish, and hardtack biscuits. The biscuits were so hard, more than one passenger lost teeth trying to tear off a morsel. Most would soak their biscuits in beer, just to be able to chew them.

There was no privacy in the passenger area, some travelers hung curtains from the ceiling in an attempt for some solitude. They all used a so called, slop jar for digestive functions. During the day, if the weather was calm, the men would dump the contents of these slop buckets over the side into the ocean. There were some rough seas during their voyage, and many became seasick, vomiting in one of these vile, foul-smelling containers or over the side of the ship. It is hard to imagine people surviving the voyage faced with meager food, smells, and not enough space for living. They had to be tough, and they just existed until they finally heard the shout from the sailor stationed in the crow's nest, "Land Ho". That had to be the most wonderful words at that time any of the survivors ever heard. Surprisingly, even with the awful conditions they had endured, only three passengers died, the oldest child of Peter and Lydia, a son, was among those that perished.

The Mayflower that carried Peter Gaunt and his family landed in the year 1636 in what month has not been determined. Nevertheless, Peter and family moved from Scituate to Lynn, and by 1637 he was one of the first settlers in Sandwich, Massachusetts. It was a small village, established in 1637, Peter Gaunt was one of the founders. Sandwich was noted for wide stretches of salt hay on the marshlands bordering the bay which gave excellent fodder for cattle, far more than the settlers could use.

Because the Massachusetts Bay Colony was land granted to the Puritans by the King of England and also because the Gaunts were excepted for transport, it is likely that Peter Gaunt was an adherent to the Puritan faith or at least passively agreed with the Puritan religious doctrine during his first years in Sandwich. The land was granted to the Puritans because they were willing to remain members of The Church of England.

When Peter and Lydia first moved to Sandwich, they only had the one child Lydia. Their first child, a boy named for his father, died on the voyage. Peter built a small board house using sawed lumber, with the help of local men. The village of Sandwich was surrounded by thick forests of trees and tools were made by the blacksmith … hammers, saws, shovels, and nails. The house was a crude dwelling with a clay and stick chimney, thatched roof and dim interior, the windows covered in oil paper, not much sunlight could enter, and the ceilings were low. It was a very depressing little house.

By 1646, Peter had become tax collector and constable and he and Lydia had increased their family by three children. He was an upstanding and important man in Sandwich and the small house, with its haphazardly added rooms for their growing family was not enough. He decided to build a larger home, a saltbox type house, typical only in New England in the 17th century. With his neighbors help, the new salt box style house was built next to the original.

The new house was two stories, small bed chambers upstairs were more like cubby holes, only used for sleeping. The whole family was busy from 'can't see to can't see', meaning sunrise to sunset. A lean-to was added to the back of the new house. The lean-to was the location where the women folk of the family, Lydia, and the daughters, would make candles, cheese, wash their clothing in wooden tubs, and brew beer. After Peter and family moved into their new home, the old original was burnt to the ground in order to collect the iron nails that were used in the building. Nails at that time were very expensive, hammered out by hand at the blacksmith's shop. The nails were then collected to be reused in another building project. The saying 'ten penny' nail originated in reference to the price.

At that time, water was frowned on as a beverage, feared to cause ailments. The family only washed their hands and feet; even children were given beer and cider on hot days beginning when they were toddlers. Their furnishings, apparel, kitchenware, and all things of importance to their survival and comfort had been transferred to their new home. This included a large Family Bible and a compass Peter had brought from England. The compass was a reminder to Peter of the voyage from England and was always an important keepsake of where he had been and in which direction he was heading. The compass was an actual artifact of Peter Gaunt's, I personally viewed the compass in the Burlington County, New Jersey Museum nearly three hundred and forty years after Peter and his family came to Plymouth Colony. That was in August 1980.

Peter Gaunt is mentioned several times in the history of Sandwich and the Bay Colonies. On the 6th of March 1638, he was fined five shillings for "being defective in arms," and on the 7th of September 1640, Peter purchased four acres of meadow land at 6 pence an acre. In 1643 the colonies of Massachusetts, Plymouth, Connecticut, and New Haven formed a confederation to take charge of Indian affairs and war matters. As a result, each colony was to support the confederation with men and money according to its military population (able bodied males between the ages of 16 and 60). In 1643, Peter Gaunt of Sandwich was listed as eligible to bear arms for New Plymouth. In 1646, Peter Gaunt was appointed constable and tax collector, both extremely important positions at the time and indicate his high standing in the colony. In 1677, Peter was appointed Surveyor of Highways, the last public office he would hold. The public office above points to the fact that Peter was actually a land surveyor.

In 1656, the Society of Friends began to appear in the colony. Many of the colony's settlers grew disenchanted with puritanism. By the early 1650's, the Puritans had firmly established a policy of calling upon the constables to act where their ministers had failed, substituting force for persuasion. Laws were enacted to impose fines for neglect of public worship, threatening corporal punishment for those who denied the "Scriptures as Life's rules" and denying citizenship to all who opposed the Puritan rule and worship.

Enforcement of such measures merely increased tensions and resistance to the Puritan church, causing many ministers to leave their churches in the colony for a calmer climate; a religious climate that upheld their right to worship as they will. The Society of Friends filled the void. As a group, the Quaker Friends had small respect for magistrates, pulpit taxes and exhibited a bravery of spirit which won many converts, including Peter Gaunt. Although the Puritans themselves came to the Massachusetts Bay Colony for freedom of worship, they would not tolerate any independence of religious views in others.

For joining the Society of Friends, Peter Gaunt also paid a price. On 2nd of March 1658, Peter, among others, had to appear in court "to answer for a tumultuous carriage at a meeting of Quakers at Sandwich… Coming before the Court with their hats on…" For this offense, he was fined 20 shillings for not taking off his hat in court, and distress to the value of 5lbs. to satisfy the fine. As a security on this debt, 5 cattle, 2 heifers, one mare, 2 three-year old steers, 8 bushels of peas, 4 bushels of Indian corn and ½ bushel of wheat were required from Peter. At a Court 13th of June 1660, George Barlow, the local constable, fined Peter Gaunt 24 lbs. At Court the 7th of May 1661, names were presented of citizens who entertained foreign Quakers at Sandwich, Peter's name was on the list, he had two that visited his home.

Many Quakers moved to Rhode Island and Long Island colonies to get away from the abusive religious practices against the Quakers in Sandwich. Finally in 1661, King Charles ordered Massachusetts to put an end to Quaker harassment. That didn't completely end the harassment of the Quakers in Sandwich. Two of Peter's sons, Hananiah and Israel had already departed to freer religious climes. In 1678, they both exchanged Sandwich land for New Jersey lands, Hananiah in Burlington County, West Jersey. No further info on where in New Jersey Israel purchased land.

The last mention of Peter Gaunt is on 10th May 1678 at the marriage of his and Lydia's, son Hananiah Gaunt to Dorothy Butler. He did not leave a will; fortunately, his wife Lydia did, naming all their children.

Children of Peter and Lydia Hampton Gaunt (from will of Lydia Hampton Gaunt, two children born in England, the rest in Sandwich, Massachusetts before 1648):

1. Peter Gaunt born in Lincolnshire, England christened the 4th of March 1634, not mentioned in Sandwich, possibly died on the voyage.
2. Lydia Gaunt born in Lincolnshire, England christened the 2nd of April 1636
3. Zachariah Gaunt born Sandwich, Massachusetts about 1639
4. Mehitable Gaunt born Sandwich, Massachusetts about 1641
5. Israel Gaunt born Sandwich, Massachusetts about 1644
6. Hananiah Gaunt born Sandwich, Massachusetts about 1647, died 1721 Burlington Co. New Jersey m. Dorothy Butler in 1678 Sandwich MM (monthly meeting)

Lydia Gaunt, Peter's daughter, married Thomas Burgess of Sandwich after 1661 as his second wife. Thomas's first wife, Elizabeth Bassett, divorced him on the 10th of June 1661, because of his adultery with Lydia Gaunt. Thomas and Lydia then married and moved to Rhode Island by 1668 where they had a son Thomas Burgess, born in Little

Compton. Lydia (Gaunt) Burgess died in 1684 in Rhode Island.

Everybody likes family stories. Here's one I have read about in my research. I don't know if it can be verified, but it is very interesting. Lydia and Thomas's divorce quite possibly was the first divorce in America! I read this somewhere, might be true, 1661 is early for a legal divorce, especially considering the position of women at that time. Elizabeth Bassett divorced him; women were not allowed to bring court proceedings and legal action.

<blockquote>
"Learning your family history is the
key to unlocking who You are"
</blockquote>

Picture of Peter's Gaunt's compass in foreground

3. Hananiah Gaunt Life in Burlington County N.J.

Hananiah Gaunt had married Dorothy Butler in 1678 at the Sandwich Friends Meeting house. Soon thereafter, they moved to Burlington County in West Jersey.

In 1685, Hananiah purchased from George Hutchinson, merchant, a tract of 500 acres of land in Burlington County. The deed states for five pounds current Boston money. Mr. Hutchinson was a merchant in Boston, Massachusetts, and I surmise the deal was struck there. The deed is signed by George Hutchinson.

The land purchased was indescribably, almost a paradise, it was in Little Egg Harbor township and had everything importance to sustain Hananiah and his family. There were marshes and waters alive with fish and various waterfowl, ducks, swans, cranes, and geese. Bays covered with shell-fish, oysters, and terrapins. The thick forests abound with red deer, bears, wolves, panthers, wild cats, foxes, rabbits, opossums, and polecats (skunks). Wild turkeys, pheasants, and quail all raised their broods in the thickets close to the ground. In the daytime, small birds enlivened the air with the music of their songs, in the twilight, whippoorwills came near and sang the twilight hours away. By midnight, hoot owls were calling back and forth to their mates from the highest branches of the tallest of trees. The citizens had to be proficient in musketry to supply food for their tables and protection from the wildest of beasts.

The first settlers appear to be people of respectability that possessed the means and enterprise necessary for establishing themselves in a new country, living in strict accordance with the discipline of the Friends society, so their descendants would have no cause to be ashamed. Most followed farming, and were skilled in blacksmithing, coopering (making wooden casks, or barrels), carpentry, shoemaking, and tanning, all being useful trades. There was a loom in every home and every family possessed a spinning wheel. There was not much time for amusements, like reading books, newspapers, or playing pianos or organs, even if the family was prosperous like Hananiah's family; there were just too many daily chores required.

Farms were important and the family applied themselves to the task of clearing their land to plant their crops. The first crops the colonists planted were Indian corn and rye, then wheat. At first, these had to be transported on the backs of horses to Mt. Holly to be ground. Soon, Mt. Holley would have its own gristmill and wagons, pulled by oxen, could move the grains.

Every husbandman planted an orchard of fruit trees, raised horses, cattle, sheep, and hogs. Hananiah planted a large orchard, apples, pears, and plums on his property.

They were very industrious indeed. An independent people, living off their land, manufacturing their own farming utensils and household furniture. After their farms were in a fair state of cultivation, owners built their dwelling, whose roofs and four sides were covered with cedar shingles or some of them 'clapboard' using iron hammered nails made with their own blacksmithing shop. Their houses were large, larger than most modern structures. Some of the clapboard houses were made of pine lumber, support beams were oak.

During the long cold winters of New England evenings, the male members of the family had employment making shoes, hoe handles, baskets, or ladles, all things that needed to be repaired or producing new ones. The female members of the house knitted, sewed, or mended what clothing was worn-out. The Juveniles were tutored by some older family members. They were taught the alphabet, spelling, how to read and write their names. Often a member of the family would read the Bible aloud, as they sat at the fireside.

Hananiah Gaunt was born in Sandwich in 1647 and married Dorothy Butler on the 10th of May 1678. He died in 1720 in Burlington County. His will is dated the 17th of July 1720.

Children of Hananiah and Dorothy Butler Gaunt (from Hananiah's will).

1. Daniel Gaunt went to the western country.
2. Zebulon Gaunt married Sophia Shrouds.
3. Mehitable Gaunt married Thomas Staple.
4. Mary Gaunt married Robert Webb.

Daniel had already received his portion of real estate, so the will only left him ten shillings, he decided to seek property elsewhere and headed west. The two girls, Mehitable and Mary, were bequeathed a part of the remainder of his personal estate, not already given to his three children, to share evenly between them. Daniel was not included.

Zebulon remained on the farm. All his father's property in Burlington County New Jersey, was left to him in his father's will. Hananiah also left ten lbs. each to his two daughters, Mehitable and Mary.

"Families are like branches on a tree. We grow in different directions yet our roots remain as one."

4. A Day on the Farm

A slither of bright orange cracked the eastern sky as Zebulon Gaunt stepped down onto the rough boards of the back porch. Spread before him were the outbuildings and cleared fields just waiting for the heavy plows. Zebulon would follow his father's example and farm this inherited land in the proper manner. Hananiah had taken good care of his land and Zebulon considered the land his legacy. He was proud of what his father had accomplished and intended to build up, not tear down, what had been entrusted to him.

Like his father, Hananiah, Zebulon was a tall, powerful man, educated in reading, writing and cipher (math skills). He had to be able to keep ledgers and figure the cost of planting and working the land. He was a plain, sincere, and earnest person. True to his Quaker faith, he was resourceful and treated all men equal. Every evening before taking to his bed, Zebulon spent an hour in quiet solitude. That was the Quaker way, in silence they worshipped God. During the day, Zebulon, his dutiful wife Sophie, and their children worked on the land.

He had rotated crops and let fields lay fallow every other year. That way the earth could rest, and the land would not turn into dry worn-out dirt. He also fertilized the land with manure from the farm animals. He turned his head and smiled at the large wooden barn where the cows, oxen, and horses lived. There was a fenced paddock for them to exercise and straw filled stalls to make them comfortable. There was also a fenced barnyard where hogs and piglets lazed in the sun or had their pink snouts poked between the fencing. Their trough was always empty. Living up to their name, they always ate like hogs. Shelled corn or kitchen slops were their usual fare, but bluntly speaking, "they would eat anything that didn't eat them first". There was a sturdy lumber barn to keep the animals warm and fed in the cold of winter. Geese, chickens, and ducks roamed free in the barnyard. There was a small building with shelves and separate boxes filled with straw providing a place for the hens to lay their eggs. The ducks and geese nested in the reeds and grasses near the three-acre pond visible from the back porch.

Zebulon had been born at Haninicon, so called by local Indians. The Quakers had no problems with the native Americans. The reason being, they treated them kindly and with deserved dignity, they were the first people that lived on the land and the Quakers recognized their status. As a tribute, Hananiah, the first owner of the five hundred acres in Burlington County, had an iron figure of an Indian affixed to the peak of their two-story barn. On rare occasions, native Americans were sighted on a distance hill, always peacefully passing by with a wave to the farmers.

Behind the Smoke house, where meat was preserved, there was a plot of ground for Mrs. Gaunt's vegetable garden; she and the daughters, Hannah, Sophie, Mary, and Dorothy were in charge of planting, picking, and preserving any vegetables not consumed by the family. During the heat of mid-summer these vegetables, fruits, and eggs were kept in the root cellar below the main house.

Zebulon had married Sophie Shrouds of Germantown, Pennsylvania. Their marriage certificate was dated Abbeyton monthly meeting on the 14th of June 1716. One of the witnesses who signed their marriage certificate was Thomas Godfrey whose wife Sarah was a sister to the bride, Sophie. Why mention this connection with Thomas Godfrey? Because he is recognized as a very important person in Pennsylvania colony. He was a glazier, a self-taught mathematician, an astronomer, inventor of the reflexing quadrant in 1730, an instrument used for navigation. He worked as a glazier and installed the glass in the Philadelphia State House, now Independence Hall. He was a friend of Benjamin Franklin, renting a house from Mr. Franklin. Franklin even described Godfrey at length in his autobiography. Thomas Godfrey was connected to the Gaunts by marriage, that connection is an illustration of how important family is and you never know what or who you will uncover. Zebulon and his family lived in the house of Hananiah until his death in 1720. When the will was proven in 1721, Zebulon became the holder of his father's property.

Children of Zebulon and Sophie Shrouds Gaunt, all born on the farm in Burlington County New Jersey:

1. Samuel Gaunt—married in 1745 to Sara Black and had two daughters, Sara Gaunt died, no verifiable date available. He remarried in 1749 to Hannah Woolman born 1726, sister of the eminent Quaker minister and journalist, John Woolman. The children of Samuel and Hannah Woolman Gaunt were Judah, Uz, Asher, Reuben, Elihu, Peter, Sarepta and Elizabeth.
2. Hannah Gaunt—married Robert Ridgeway of Little Egg Harbor.
3. Mary Gaunt—married Jacob Gamble of Bordentown New Jersey.
4. Zebulon Gaunt Jr.—born 1720 on his father's farm Springfield Township, Burlington, County N.J. On 16th November 1750 in Christ's Church Philadelphia, he married Esther Woolman born 1730, sister to Hannah Woolman (mentioned above) in plainer language, brothers Samuel and Zebulon Jr. married sisters Hannah and Esther Woolman
5. Sophia Gaunt married Daniel Mathis in 1743.
6. Israel Gaunt born between 1725-1730 in Springfield Township, Burlington County.
7. Dorothy Gaunt married Joshua Teague, probably in the Carolinas, she is mentioned in letters written between the three brothers after they separated.

Samuel, Zebulon Jr. and Israel Gaunt had a strong affection for each other. When Zebulon Jr., Israel, and two of the sisters left New Jersey for the Carolinas, the three brothers decided to add an extra T to their surname so that the descendants of the New Jersey Gaunts would be known to each other. The surname than became Gauntt. Today the descendants of the New Jersey branch in South Carolina spell their name Gantt.

To my readers, I know the names are confusing and repetitious. I have collected this information and studied these people for many years, and it is still mind boggling to me.

<blockquote>
"Genealogy: Where you confuse the
dead and irritate the living."

—Unknown
</blockquote>

This is so true! I guess you have to really care about where you came from to know where you are going. People who do genealogical research have to be dedicated to confusion and conjecture, with a willingness to be proven wrong, only with definitive evidence.

Gauntt home in New Jersey called Haninicon

5. Down the Great Wagon Road to the Carolinas

The sun was just beginning to rise in the east, golden light touched the tops of the pine forest in the distance and ran across the brown fields. The tall grandfather clock in the hallway below began to clang the hour. After each clang there was an audible quiver that could be heard rushing through the air. Esther climbed from the feather bed and slipped her feet into warm woolen slippers and her arms into the sleeves of her dressing gown. The first thing she noticed was her husband Zeb Jr. was gone from their bed.

The clock resounded the time, it was six o'clock, barely daylight outside as she headed down the stairs. Midway down she could hear the low whisper of voices coming from the kitchen and saw a sliver of light from the cracked kitchen door reflecting on the polish wood of the hall below. It was spring, early April 1753 and three covered wagons stood silent in the backyard of the great house.

The wagons were loaded with all the necessary foodstuffs, dried fruit, potatoes, and onions from the root cellar, salt, flour, pepper, coffee, and tea. A trunk of clothing pushed to the front inside and bedding tucked next to the trunks. There was very little furniture, just stools and a small table within easy reach for sitting up camp in the evenings. There was a wooden box attached to the outside, filled with an iron skillet, large iron pot with lid, tin cups, plates and eating utensils, pottery bowls for stirring and mixing for the womenfolk to cook their supper in the evenings. Cooking would have to be done over an open fire requiring iron rods to hold the pot above the flames, meat could be cooked on a spit or fried in the iron skillet. Barrels of water, a long dipper hanging beside each, and a spare wheel attached to the outside of the wagon bed, also oil lanterns hung from nails on the boards of the wagon base. The men intended to use their muskets to supplement meat. Two hams, smoked sausage, and a haunch of beef were already in a barrel covered with salt in the middle wagon. Any tools they might need were stored underneath the wagon seat where they sat. There would be small villages along their journey and solitary traders where needed supplies could be purchased. It was the backcountry, but not the wilderness completely devoid of people.

The noise of low voices came from Zebulon Sr. and his three sons, Samuel, Zeb Jr., and Israel discussing the monumental trip to the South that the two brothers and their two sisters, Sophie Mathis and Dorothy were about to embark on. The siblings had made the decision to seek their fortune in the south. The homeplace, Haninicon would be left to the oldest son, Samuel, and the will of Zebulon Sr. would be executed by their sister, Mary Gamble, when the time came. The other siblings were well aware of the plans for the land in Burlington County. The trip to Orange County, North Carolina would take about a month's travel down the Great Wagon Road. It was the most popular trail to take from Pennsylvania southward after 1744. As soon as the travelers crossed into North Carolina, the road name would change to The Carolina road and go through Salisbury chartered 1753 and Charlottetown settled about 1750. It began as an Indian path and was broadened by the felling of trees as pioneers began to travel southward.

This day in April would most probably be their last goodbye. It was not a sad day for any of the brothers and they held no ill will towards their father, Zebulon. The oldest son always inherited the farm. They were a close family and the younger, Zeb Jr. and Israel looked upon this trip as a grand adventure. They would stay in touch through letters, even though they would, by necessity, be few and far between. There was no regular mail service in 1753, letters had to be sent by someone traveling back and forth along the wagon road.

The trip to North Carolina would not be an easy one, but the travelers were excited as they climbed onto the wagon seats. Zeb Jr. and Esther were in the first wagon, Sophie and husband, Daniel Mathis occupied the middle, and brother Israel and his sister Dorothy brought up the rear. All wagons were carrying muskets, plenty of gun powder and musket balls, enough to hunt along the way and for protection from marauders and Indians. The eastern Cherokees in North Carolina had been forced to cede their land to the colonists and there had been armed conflict along the road. The bigger threat would come from thieves and bandits.

Each night they would stop at a clearing near the road, the men taking turns standing watch. Their destination was New Garden monthly meeting in Orange County, North Carolina. Whether they would settle there was still yet to be decided.

"It is not easy to be a pioneer—but
oh, it is Fascinating."

—Elizabeth Blackwell

*Mrs. Gauntt standing in front of grandfather
clock that stood in the hall at Haninicon.*

6. Letters From Home

I have been very fortunate to have letters that my Burlington County, New Jersey relatives preserved, and which I
transcribed years ago. They were all written from the south
to Samuel and family and date from 1753 to 1779. Evidently no letters that our northern relatives sent to Israel,
Zeb Jr., Sophia, or Dorothy have survived. I'm sure they
replied to these letters, but I have not been able to locate
them.

Two hundred years after they, Zeb Jr., Israel, Sophia,
and Dorothy emigrated to South Carolina, I contacted our
family in New Jersey. To me this is a fascinating story. I
had seen references for Peter Gaunt from England. I was
very much into genealogy but had no idea the extent of
my New Jersey family's collection of original documents.
What research I had done revealed that the Gauntts were
Quakers, also called Friends, and lived in New England,
but I didn't understand how I was related to the Quaker
Gauntts in New Jersey.

I wrote a letter to Swarthmore college in Pennsylvania

where the Friends Historical library is located. In January 1980, I received a reply, stating they did not do personal genealogy research, but included with their note was a list of local researchers who could be hired to research the Friends records. Along with the note was a newspaper copy full page entitled 'Jefferson Gauntt And The Saga Of Haninicon'. There were paragraphs outlined with red pencil speaking of the letters and documents still in the family, including a picture of the house owned by Edwin A. Gauntt.

The name of the newspaper was the Mount Holly Herald. It had no date at the top, so I had no idea when the article had been published. In 1980, there was no internet or smart phones, so I wrote a letter to the newspaper referencing the article and the person who wrote it. After, possibly a month I received a letter from Mrs. Gertrude Gauntt, widow of Edwin A. Gauntt. She was most gracious and agreed to share any copies I would be interested in and invited me to come visit her.

In August of 1980, a great aunt, my sister Louise, and her husband Arnold, two of my daddy's 1st cousins, Cleola, and Barbara, myself and two youngsters, Aimee, and Mary Ann, piled into the huge Chevrolet Impala station wagon belonging to Arnold and Louise. Arnold was at the wheel as we backed out of their dirt driveway. Directly in front and visible through the windshield were tall junipers dark and grey growing beside the stream called Coon Branch. These tall trees were framed by a sky of orange, with small fluffy clouds lined by glowing bright sunlight.

Leaving before dawn, we were traveling all day up I- 95,

stopping at Quantico, Virginia to eat lunch. I can't remember a lot of particulars (it's only been almost 44 years). I do remember Aunt Eva (widow of my grandfather Gantt's brother, Woodard) made fried apple pies, homemade biscuits, and fried chicken to eat in the car. Cleola, my daddy's first cousin, had a glass of wine in the motel room that night and fell off the bed (not because of the wine).

We spent the next day with Mrs. Gertrude Gauntt, took pictures of the outside of the family home, Haninicon (no longer owned by the family), visited the Burlington County museum (where a compass belonging to Peter Gaunt was on display), and stopped by the large farmhouse in Jobstown, N.J. where Mrs. Caroline Gauntt Armstrong and husband, Russell, lived.

After spending the day in Burlington County, we dropped by Washington, DC on the way home (my very first visit to our nations' Capitol). On the road again heading south on I-95, Arnold called Daddy's 1st cousin, Cy Gantt, from a pay phone. Cy suggested we meet him for supper. We met him at a nice restaurant in Willington, Delaware, spending an enjoyable evening of wonderful food and marvelous conversation. I believe it was a long weekend, Thursday through Sunday. I know it was memorable and very busy! That's how I got copies of the letters.

Just think, if you could read letters that your fifth great grandfather had written expressing his thoughts, his hopes, dreams, his experiences, the description and location of his land. No one needs to be an historian to appreciate the contents of such letters. I am a direct descendant of Israel Gauntt, a patriot in the American Revolution. Because Israel was a member of the Quaker faith, he was more of a pacifist. However, he supported independence from Great Britain. He supported the fight by donating feed for horses and food for the men who were fighting in the trenches, so to speak. He was an American patriot!

Some excerpts from the original letters: I will reference from the originals, names, dates, and content, but have decided to use the correct modern English spellings of what they are intending. It will be easier for my readers to understand the meaning of their words in these letters, spelling has definitely changed in the last two hundred years, they will be listed chronologically, from the earliest date. Every letter, no exceptions, starts out expressing concerns about health, sending love to all family members, and urging the recipient to write as soon as possible. The first couple paragraphs begin to be so repetitious, I have decided to be very selective as to the parts I share. But be aware they were loving and compassionate about family, I just decided to not report those parts at the expense of being monotonous or downright boring.

1st day 6th month 1753
Orange County, North Carolina at the head of Deep river

To Samuel Gauntt from Zebulon, Esther, and Israel Gauntt the Quaker settlement by friends called New Garden. I have the opportunity to send thee a few lines loving brother and sister Samuel and Hannah by which you may understand that we are all in good health at this time, hoping that this may find you in good health also which we give our kind love to you all father, mother, brothers, and sisters. I hope that you may not forget us although we are separated here in this world. I hope we may all live a life that we may meet together in the world where we may never part and rest from our labors. These lines from Zebulon (this is Zebulon Jr.), Esther, and Israel Gauntt.

Postscript, We do desire thee as brothers in love Samuel Gauntt that if thee have an opportunity to send our certificates and direct them to New Garden Monthly Meeting the County and province above said and if they could be sent to John Allen at Gottengin (maybe a local village). I believe we may readily get them by reason that there are people traveling backwards and forwards. (Since Zebulon Sr. did not die until 1772, the reference to love sent to Father and Mother implies that both their parents Zebulon and Sophie Shrouds Gauntt were still alive).

20th day of 5th month 1754

Loving brother Samuel Gauntt, I write a few lines to let thee know I have received thy letter, and thy hope and love was well excepted. I think it's right for me to give an account of the country, which I think I could for I have been in most all parts of North Carolina government. Our brother, Zebulon Jr. has a mind to come into your parts and he can give the account of the country as well as I can. Lately Daniel Mathis has come into our parts (referring to where they reside) he is in poor circumstances. Thy loving and affectionate brother Israel Gaunt.

(The siblings resided in North Carolina, maybe two years before moving further south into South Carolina, It appears Zebulon Jr. was planning a trip back to N.J.)

7th day 10th month 1754

From Monthly Meeting of Friends in Burlington to Friends at their Monthly Meeting at New Garden NC, Samuel Gauntt wishes to reside among you for some part of the ensuing winter in order to assist his brother in some necessary affairs.

(Samuel Gauntt plans to go south for the winter, he probably was intending to help Zebulon to build his grist mill, at least five months elapsed between this correspondence saying Samuel was going to New Garden, NC meeting and the time Zeb Jr., Esther, and Israel arrived home from the Woolman's. A lot can change in five months).

25th day 3rd month 1755

Send you a few lines, to let ye know that we arrived safe home and found all in good health. Do not forget to write to us when time and opportunity may permit our kind love to you all.

Zebulon Jr., Esther, and Israel Gauntt

We arrived at home in 5 weeks and a day from mother

Woolman's. My mill is not built. (mother Woolman would be mother of Zeb Jr.'s wife, Esther, the Woolmans lived in Pennsylvania). It seems that Samuel and Zeb Jr. were at cross purposes with the coming and going. According to a later letter, Zeb Jr. built his grist mill in Camden, SC and was working for Joseph Kershaw. I guess the time lapse of months between the letters could explain the confusion.

8th day of the 2nd month, 1762 (a lapse of almost seven years)
Wateree River, St. Johns Parish

To Samuel, we are in good health sending you wishes of the same. I have five children. Israel, wife, and children are well, sister Sophia is dead, died the 12th day of the 12th month 1761. (Zeb Jr and Sophia Gauntt Mathis and their families were definitely in Camden by this time, Sophia is interred in the Quaker Cemetery in Camden SC, the announcement of Sophia death seems a little abrupt to me, but I guess there's no gentle way to put it.) Zeb Jr. continues, I do verily believe that she (Sophia) has made a good end, she being sick about 24 days. No more at present but our kind love to all.

(Zeb's letter to Samuel continues with some directions for sending letters in reply). If thy please, leave the letters at Benjamin Shoemaker in Philadelphia to be directed to Aaron Lowcock in Charles Town for Joseph Kershaw at Pine Tree Hill. Kershaw is a merchant which I am in his employ and hath been for 2 years past. Now I have under-taken to build him a sawmill and a grist mill, which I and

Israel Hall join him in partnership on the Congaree River where we shall float our boards to Charles Town.

Postscript—I desire that thee would undertake to make a set of wagon wheels 4 ft by 4 inches high and 5 ft 4 inches and make them as strong as ever thy had made, have them delivered to Benjamin Shoemaker in Philadelphia and he will pay thee for them, let it be more or less, and run a bed on the wheels. That I may know the wheels when they come. There being 5 sets of wheels sent to Philadelphia. These wheels being for my friend, Joseph Kershaw. Signed Zeb Gauntt Jr.

(folded letter addressed on the back to Samuel Gauntt in West New Jersey Burlington County, Township of Springfield) sealed with wax and personal stamp visible.

5th day 1st month 1764

To Uriah Woolman

Having left my family 3 days ago in company with my beloved friend and cousin, William Hunt. Signed Zeb Gauntt Jr.

Postscript If Thee have any mind to write direct thy letter to Aaron Lowcock in Charles Town for Joseph Kershaw at Pine Tree, I have 6 children, 4 sons Nebo, Zimri, Samuel, Issachar, 2 daughters Beulah, and Caronhappuck.

30th day 12th month 1769

To Sam Gauntt in West Jersey

Sending love to all the family and wishing good health.

Post Script. I heard lately from brother Israel and family. They were in reasonable health. I was lately at Sister Dorothy's. She has six children, her husband's name is Joshua Teague, children names, Elijah, Israel, William, Abner, Isabella, and Rebekah.

Zeb Jr

30th December 1771

Loving brother Samuel Gauntt

We are all well, Sister Dorothy and her family are well. I now follow farming in South Carolina, West Broad, and Saluda Rivers. I do not expect to come to these parts anymore. I have received a letter from thee and am glad to hear of thy welfare. Remembering my love to our Father and Mother and to thee and thy family.

Israel Gauntt

Sister Dorothy is living about 10 miles from me Zebulon 70 miles.

26th of 10th month 1772 To Samuel

Love and good health wished to all your family.

P.S. My family being well, some of my children are suffering from chills and fever at present. Our kind love to all. Zeb Gauntt

29th day of 7th month 1778

Dear Brother and Sister Samuel and Hannah Gauntt, having an opportunity to send a few lines by two friends the name of Latham (surname) at these troublesome times. My family is through mercy in reasonable health at present, all that are at home except one of my sons who hath been ailing for some time but through mercy is amending. My two eldest sons are gone a trading with a load of indigo to Maryland or Pennsylvania. Nebo and Zimri and their eldest sister, Beulah, went with them as far as New Garden and we have not heard from them for near three months. I heard from brother Israel a few days past. He and his family were reasonably well, and I should be very glad to hear from thee and thy family.

This from thy affectionate Brother Zeb Gauntt Jr.

Post Script. A few lines from thee would be very acceptable in these trying times which I believe is too many.

21st day 6th month 1779

To Samuel Gauntt

Dear Brother, having an opportunity to send a few lines by friend Richard Price of Philadelphia, which I give thee to understand something of our situation at present. We are living at the old place near Camden at the ferry, a very troublesome place with soldiers day and night. My wife and Zimri and Samuel are in a poor state of health at present, the rest in a middling state of health, which I hope these may find thee and thine in the same. It is very troublesome times. The English army lying near Charles Town which they have a great call for men. They fined me and my son, Samuel, 500 lbs. each and took from us to the value of 2000 dollars and now the law is more severe, no fines but the body. The Captain came and took my eldest sons, Nebo and Zimri, and kept them traveling for near 300 hundred miles until their feet were very blistered and obliged to walk in that condition for some days so that they suffered very much in diverse ways, and were detained near 6 weeks and then Colonel Kershaw interceded with the president and they being both millwrights he got them discharged in order to repair and attend them for the law excuses none but millers and ferrymen, so that the officers are sending of summons for myself and son, Sam. So, except for some power comes to rule shortly we need not expect nothing else but to be taken, there being 15 or 16 from Bush River, Long Cane, and George, them 3 meetings and some of them in Charles Town under a guard. I was not long since at Brother Israel's and Sister Dorothy's, and they and their family were in reasonable health. If I remember our sister has 4 sons and 3 daughters. This is from thy loving brother Zeb Gaunt.

The letters are very fascinating, especially those later ones that speak of the troublesome times and the Revolutionary War. Colonel Kershaw of Revolutionary War fame had his home commandeered by Cornwallis for his headquarters during the Battle of Camden. His wife, Sarah Mathis Kershaw was the daughter of Sophia Gauntt Mathis, sister to my 5th great grandfather and Revolutionary patriot, Israel Gauntt. Colonel Kershaw was a good friend and employer of Zeb Gauntt Jr., brother of my ancestor, Israel. The Revolutionary Park outside of Camden includes a house built on the original foundation of Colonel and Mrs. Kershaw's home, this house is now called the Cornwallis house.

Colonel Kershaw of Camden was not the only Revolutionary hero to come from the Mathis/Gauntt union. Daniel and Sophie's children were ardent patriots. Besides Sarah mentioned above, their daughter Mary Mathis married Captain William Nettles. Captain Nettles was born the 2nd of April 1734 and died the 15th of October 1832 at the age of 98 years (dates from his tombstone in the Quaker cemetery in Camden). According to Captain Nettles pension application, he was active from the commencement of our Revolutionary struggle to the end of the war. The greater part of his service he bore the rank of Captain. He served under Generals Sumter, Marion, and Benjamin Lincoln. Near the end of the war, he followed General Greene to Eutaw Springs. He states he was actively engaged and constantly on duty. When he applied for a pension, he stated he was in his 86th year, had raised a numerous family who have become greatly dispersed, and is left alone to support himself. Captain Nettles states he has become very infirm and is greatly in need of his country's assistance. Sixteen citizens who knew nothing of his service signed the pension application, "but from the general report, we cheerfully sign, subscribe our names to the truth of his excellent character." I would think, Captain Nettles deserved a pension, the first signature on his application was Thomas Sumter, Revolutionary General famously called "The Fighting Gamecock!" That signature alone should have guaranteed his pension.

Israel Mathis, brother of Sarah and Mary, practiced law at Camden in partnership with his brother, Samuel, until 1810, when he moved to Sumter County.

Samuel Mathis (1760-1823) was the first white male born on Camden soil, Despite being a Quaker, he enlisted in his brother-in-law Joseph Kershaw's militia, he was captured and paroled in 1780. He broke parole in 1781 and fought with General Francis Marion. As far as the claim of being the first white male, girls didn't count, neither did other races, his brother Israel may have been younger.

According to a letter written to their kinfolk in West Jersey, Sophie Mathis, mother of Samuel died in 1761. According to the copy of the original letter Sophia died the 12th day of the 12th month 1761, being sick 24 days. It is sad to think, she never saw how important her children became in the founding of our country.

"A strong family is the glue binding
each individual to the world."

Caroline Gauntt Armstrong and Gertrude H. Gauntt, wife of Edwin A. Gauntt

The Gauntt home, Haninicon

7. South Carolina in the Revolution — Battleground of Freedom

There is no argument against the designation of South Carolina as 'The Battleground of Freedom'. There were more than 200 battles fought in this state during the American Revolution, more than any other state/colony, beginning in November 1775 at Ninety Six's Star fort. Battles with unrecognizable names like Gowen's Fort, Turkey Creek, Fork of the Edisto, Deans Swamp, Galley Fight, and Pon Pon. (I later found that Pon Pon was the Indian name for Edisto).

Battles named, Salkehatchie, Choctawhatchee Combahe, Wadboo, Tomassy, and Cherokee Ford immediately elicit visions of native Americans just by hearing the names, battles like Schooner Rattlesnake, Cunningham's Raid, Hell Hole Creek, and Buford's Massacre sound ominous. Some were just considered skirmishes, others deciding the course of the United States and our freedoms. There is no doubt the Revolution was won here.

The first battle fought in an attempt to occupy Charleston was the Battle of Sullivan's Island on June 28, 1776. The walls were being constructed before the battle took place of Palmetto logs, the most plentiful trees available. Those Palmetto logs became the deciding factor between success and failure. The walls were constructed with the fibrous and spongy logs of the Palmetto. When the British fired their cannons, the cannon balls were almost absorbed into the logs or repelled. During the battle, cannon balls literally bounced off the wall of the constructed barriers. The first fort was called Fort Sullivan. The Palmetto logs inspired the flag and nickname of South Carolina, as "The Palmetto State". The fort was renamed for the U.S. patriot commander, Colonel William Moultrie. The battle was a stunning victory for the patriots. Today, June 28 is still celebrated as Carolina Day in South Carolina.

The afore mentioned battle was one of many victories for the Americans, each having some important meaning. The Battle of Yamacraw Bluff on the Savannah River, March 2-3, 1776, because it ended British control in the colony of Georgia. In many battles, Continental troops and militia fought side by side against the hordes of British redcoats.

Great battles that decided the course of liberty from Britain include, King's Mountain on October 7th, 1780, fought entirely by citizen soldiers, the Overmountain men from North Carolina, crushed the Loyalists in the region. Major Patrick Ferguson who recruited loyalists in the backcountry was attacked by local militia and killed on King's Mountain.

The night before the Battle of Cowpens, Daniel Morgan, known as the 'old Wagoneer' spread the word for all militia to rendezvous at the Cowpens. The battle would be fought in an area 500 yards wide and the same in length near present day Spartanburg, South Carolina. It was devoid of undergrowth with few trees. The trees were mainly large oak and pines. Colonists grazed their cattle here in the springtime, but it was the 17th of January and bitterly cold. In the springtime the large oaks provided shade for the grazing animals, now only a few dried leaves were left clinging to the branches dancing in the wind. The patriot militia camped between two low hills on this almost barren stretch of land. Soon a very important battle would rage on this land. Through the night, Overmountain men familiar with the terrain and Andrew Pickens militia drifted into camp. That night they squatted around fires and rolled up in their woolen blankets. Morgan drifted among the campfires and offered encouragement to the men; his speeches spoke of current patriot victories and the importance of the coming battle. He spoke the language of these patriots, and they listened, aware of his past exploits in the French and Indian wars and as the hero of the Battle of Saratoga. All were in good spirits and ready to fight the British. It was noted by his men, Morgan did not sleep a wink that night.

A grey dawn broke clear and freezing, the breath of all patriots hung in the air. The redcoats, which included the hated Banastre Tarleton, were aligned shoulder to shoulder marching toward the American forces. When the musket fire and cannon begin to roar, smoke was so thick, it was hard to distinguish the patriots, easier to see the marching British in there bright red coats. Morgan had aligned his men in three sections, sharpshooters were out-front hiding behind trees and picking off the officers. As Morgan's militia moved forward, they dodged behind trees and parried saber slashes with their rifles. The battle was over in less than an hour.

I recall rules for the Revolution, put forth by a stand-up comedian, I can't remember the comedian's name, but he said the number one rule and most important, was the British had to wear redcoats and march shoulder to shoulder towards the Americans. The second, just as important as the 1st, the Americans were to hide behind rocks and trees, shoot the redcoats at will, and they could dress in any color that allowed them to blend in with the landscape. I believe those rules were followed at Cowpens.

In 1779-80 British redcoats came south in mass, defeating and capturing much of the southern Continental Army. In the back country, it was neighbor against neighbor, Tories, like Robert Cunningham and Moses Kirkland who remained loyal to the English. Cunningham, especially, was vicious toward the patriots, patriots who were willing to do anything to support the cause of Independence. Great patriot leaders in South Carolina, Andrew Pickens, Thomas Sumter, and of course General Francis Marion. Daniel Morgan, the hero of the Cowpens, the old Wagoneer, as he was called since he hauled wagonloads of supplies over the mountains to settlers and during the French and Indian War in the 1750's. Morgan even referred to himself as 'the old wagoner'.

Nathaniel Greene won at Guildford Courthouse in North Carolina in March 1781, then Greene moved into

South Carolina. Cornwallis headed north to Virginia. Greene's decision to turn southward allowed British control of the south to unravel, it seemed to be a diversionary move leading Cornwallis to Yorktown. Nathaniel Greene was a Quaker and was revered after his victory, even though he had actually been voted 'out of unity' with the Quaker faith, that was forgotten, and he was embraced as being a Friend.

A battle was fought between Patriots and Loyalists near current Batesburg-Leesville in October of 1781. The location is past I-20, a little north of highway 178. The battle was at a place called Hartley's but was renamed in 1781 as 'Hell Hole Creek' because of the magnitude of evil and savagery in which the patriots were murdered. There were 28 patriots killed by 'Bloody Bill Cunningham' and his band of murderous followers. Not only were the patriots killed, but their bodies were also dismembered and mutilated. Supposedly, later this site would be near the homeplace of Soloman and Dolly Gantt Altman. So ironic, I have passed this area numerous times, in my life, never knowing what actually happened not 100 yards from Hwy. 178.

Patriots did not actually have to fight in a battle and carry a musket to be considered a Revolutionary patriot. My Revolutionary ancestor, Israel Gauntt of Newberry provided provisions and forage for the militia's use in 1779, 1780, 1782 and 1783. The value of his contributions amounted to nineteen lbs. four shillings and nine pence farthing sterling.

A story printed in the Annals of Newberry by Judge John O'Neal and John Chapman deals with my ancestor,

Israel Gauntt, and an attempted attack on his family by a tory marauder, I will report here the story as originally written.

"A man named Hubbs, who served with the bloody tory and renegade Cunningham in South Carolina was an 'out-lier' during the war. At one time he proposed, with two confederates, to rob an old man of Quaker habits—Israel Gauntt—who was reputed to be in possession of money. The three rode up one evening and asked for lodging, which was refused. Hubbs rode to the kitchen door, in which Mrs. Gauntt was standing, and asked for water. He sprang in while she turned to get the water, and as she handed it to him, she saw his arms. Her husband, informed of this, secured the doors. Hubbs presented his pistol at him; but his deadly purpose was frustrated by the old man's daughter, Hannah. She threw up the weapon, and, being of masculine proportions and strength, grappled with and threw him to the floor, where she held him, though wounded by his spurs—in spite of his desperate struggles—till he was disabled by her father's blows. Gauntt was wounded through the window by Hubbs companion, and another ball grazed his heroic daughter just above the eye; but both escaped without further injury. Hannah afterwards married a man named Mooney. The gentleman (Judge O'Neal) who relates the foregoing incident has often seen her and describes her as one of the kindest and most benevolent of women. She died at the age of fifty and her grandson, a worthy and excellent man is now living in the village of Newberry.

The children of Israel and Hannah Spencer Gauntt (named in Israel's will written December 25, 1798, filed in Newberry Courthouse and recorded May 15, 1800:) Hannah Spencer Gauntt, had one daughter by her first marriage, Susanah Coate. Hannah Gauntt's will dated 15th day of August 1813. Hannah left the house in Newberry to her son Jacob and two acres of land.

1. James Gauntt, born the 7th of September 1765, married Elizabeth Mills.
2. Joseph Gauntt, born about 1770, died 1816 married Bathsheba.
3. Jacob Gauntt, his estate settled 1836, married Mary Echols.
4. Hannah Gauntt, born ca 1774, married a man named Mooney.
5. Rebecca Gauntt, born ca 1776, married Thomas Gilbert.
6. Mary Gauntt, born ca 1778.

My direct ancestor, Joseph Gauntt, married a woman named Bathsheba, he died in 1816 and Bathsheba remarried Benjamin Stubbs.

When Israel Gauntt of Newberry died in 1800, he left to son, Joseph "to my beloved son Joseph, I give a tract of land on the waters of the Edisto the place where he now lives containing 100 acres" date of will 25th of December 1798. This land was in Lexington County, SC. In Newberry County land records Israel bought these 100 acres in 1788 from Samuel Rawls. It is described as a tract of land in the county of Lexington afore said on the waters of the Edisto River a branch thereof called Chinkepin Creek, between Black Creek and Lightwood knot Bridge creek bounding on all sides by vacant land. Joseph Gauntt and his family moved into Lexington District between 1788 and 1798.

"Tough Times Never Last, But Tough People Do"

—Dr Robert Schuller

Gauntt house, Newberry SC, 45 & 46 are also the same building. The oldest building still standing, belonged to Jacob Gauntt, son of Revolutionary patriot, Israel Gauntt.

8. Joseph Gauntt, Life in Lexington County, S.C.

There was a chill in the autumn air, it was late evening, the darkness was coming fast, settling like a grey blanket over the little town. The three sons of Israel: James, Jacob, and Joseph were playing a game snuggled in thick wool coats, collars turned up and woolen lined leather gloves on their hands. The last rays of the sun were vanishing fast, along with the view of Newberry from the front yard of their home on College Street. Three brothers were enjoying the evening air, playing a game of hide and seek before the darkness drove them inside. Joseph, a young lad of eleven, could see the glare of the oil lamps atop their posts. The streetlamps were lit every evening at five o'clock sharp by Mr. Webb. After the lamps were burning, he helped his wife close up the millinery shop and escorted her to their home. The street lights illuminated the way for folks hurrying home from their jobs in the little town — the butcher, shopkeepers, shoemaker, carpenter, and the blacksmith. Without the oil lamps it would be pitch black. After leaving Main Street, they could find their way by the window lights of their neighbors' homes or, if need be, a torch. A wooden match with sulfur on the end struck against the rough boards of the covered walk immediately lit a blaze on the hand held torch.

Joseph, James, and Jacob paused their play, in the distance they heard yelling and galloping hoof beats. As the rider came closer, the boys could recognize the man's voice. "That's Mr. Dooley!" Jacob exclaimed excitedly. They, the three, realized immediately this must be important news. Isaac Dooley was the 'town crier', it was his paid duty to walk about the town and announce news to the townspeople. In this case, Mr. Dooley wasn't walking about town and ringing a bell to alert the folks. He was riding 'hell bent for leather' at breakneck speed, everyone should stay clear, some really important news was being shouted.

As he came closer, the boys could understand what all the yelling was about, "Cornwallis surrendered his army to General Washington on the 19th at Yorktown, Virginia, the war is over!" Holding the reins with his left hand, he waved quickly at the three boys and continued on his route through the town. This was wonderful news. People immediately began to gather in small groups on the main street to share their thoughts, including Israel and Hannah Gauntt. The grownups realized it would still take much time for the British to depart from the colonies. More violent skirmishes between the patriots and the Tories would still be fought; men would die, but this was most certainly great news, the British had been defeated!

The three sons of Israel and Hannah Spencer Gauntt

would always remember Mr. Dooley and the sound of his horse's hoofbeats on that chilly October night in 1781.

It was a story they would proudly share with their children and grandchildren.

Joseph Gauntt was born in Newberry, South Carolina but would not die in the little town. When his father, Israel Gauntt passed away, he left one hundred acres of land to Joseph stating, "the place where he now lives," in Lexington District. Joseph moved there between 1788 and 1798, Israel died in 1800, but Joseph knew that would be his part of his father's estate and Israel had consented to Joseph moving there before he died, the actual will made it legal and binding.

* * * * *

Joseph's wife, Sarah, and their three young children traveled to Lexington County in the spring of 1798, wild dogwoods were just beginning to bloom beside the road, and yellow jasmine perfumed their weary travel with sweet fragrance. Their two covered wagons were pulled by strong, steady oxen. The roads in the back country were very sandy, at places deep sand beds hindered travel. Oxen were built for pulling heavy loads and could easily navigate through the deep sandy soil and they were not as excitable as horses or mules. The second wagon was driven by Dave Brown, his wife Mary and their teenage son, Alfred (Al), all occupied the thick board seat.

The Brown family had been servants in Joseph's home in Newberry for four years. He hired them for low wages but also guaranteed them shelter, food, and a little plot of their own for a vegetable garden. Dave and Al would help Joseph with the farm, for which Joseph had promised to build the Brown family a small house. Mary Brown had agreed to help Mrs. Gauntt with the housework and cooking. Joseph's other children rode with the Browns in the second wagon, except for Jacob, the oldest son at almost eight years, he rode on the back of one of the five horses trailing behind the second wagon. The Brown family were comfortable working for Joseph, he was not too demanding, and Dave, Mary, and their son looked upon the Gauntts more as friends than employers. They reached the North Edisto River, traveling parallel beside the black water on an old Indian trail. Dave and his son Al chopped down any undergrowth that hindered their wagons. When they reached Chinkepin creek that flowed into the Edisto, they crossed over at a shallow ford.

Joseph's father, Israel, purchased the property from Samuel Rawls on the 16th day of January 1788. Rawls had acquired the one hundred acres by a certain grant from his excellency, William Bull Esquire, Lieutenant Governor and Commander in Chief over the province of South Carolina on the 8th of March 1765. Samuel Rawls and his family had built a large clapboard house on the property plus barns and outbuildings. Also mentioned in the deed of sale to Israel Gauntt was timber, meadows, pastures, orchards, ponds, lakes, and fishing ways. The whole kit and kaboodle was listed as being conveyed, released, and confirmed to Israel Gauntt for the sum of thirty-five pounds, fourteen shillings, and three pence sterling money. The plantation or tract of land containing one hundred acres lying and being on the waters of the Edisto River a branch thereof called Chinkepin Creek.

One hundred acres was a large piece of land to begin a new life on. The whole family was pleased with the scenery, the river, creek, and the variety of trees, mostly oak, pine, walnut, sycamore, and pecan. They set tents up beside the wagons in a clearing about one hundred yards from Chinkepin creek. Joseph carried a copy of the land survey map that had been filed when Israel had purchased the land from Samuel Rawls. He could tell where the lines were and where they had set up their camp.

This was the first time Joseph and family had laid eyes on the property and were pleasantly surprised the house Samuel Rawls had built was sound, there was even a small cabin for the Browns. There were fields, once cleared, and a big barn for their animals. The yard and about the house had brambles and tall weeds that would need chopping and burning in piles. The fields were grown-up with pine saplings, but no large trees had to be taken down. The terraces between the fields would need repair, heavy rain had washed some of the height away. These tasks would require hard work, but it was far better than starting from scratch. In the house and cabin, heavy cobwebs needed to be swept away from ceilings, corners, and window seals and the board floors were thick with sand and grit. The few broken pieces of furniture left by the previous occupants could be added to their fires. Rudimentary furniture could be built to supplement the few pieces in their two wagons. Joseph was exceptionally good at carpentry and with Dave and

Al's help, they would have the necessary pieces of furniture in no time.

Joseph and Dave would spend a couple of weeks getting to know the lay of the land, how plentiful were deer, rabbits, squirrels, and turkey, all animals they would hunt for food, there were also dangerous animals in the surrounding forest, wolves, bobcats, and panthers. They had to be cautious and keep their muskets handy at all times. How many other creeks and springs were on the land, and how thick and what kind of trees made up the forest? They would camp here and make daily trips, hunting and familiarizing themselves with the view and landscape of the property. Sarah and Mary would stay busy with sweeping and cleaning. They would, out of necessity, have to make a trip back to Newberry, or Camden to purchase nicer furniture, dishes, and linens. But that could wait until they were settled in and had cleaned the buildings of cobwebs and left over debris.

The soil was of special importance since they intended to farm as their major source of revenue. Joseph and Dave had agreed the soil was excellent for raising most crops, and the pastureland, most already fenced with split rails, was adequate for the oxen and horses. They would need to buy some chickens and hogs, but there were neighbors not more than a day's ride that might be willing to sell what animals they required.

The men folk loaded their muskets and headed into the surrounding forest to hunt for their supper. Jeb's teenage son Al would stay and protect the women and children.

After searching the whole of the one hundred acres,

Joseph and Dave found a beautiful spot not two hundred yards from the black waters of the Edisto river. It was not swampy here, mostly oaks and juniper grew all the way down to the river. There was also a rocky spot where a couple of good size boulders rested among the trees. Here the water of the Edisto flowed in a lazy way and was shallow enough to ford by wagon or on horseback. Joseph and Dave immediately built a bridge across for human traffic, a log foot bridge. They cut a good size oak, propping it on a large boulder, they were able to use axes, wedges, and mauls to split the trunk. The oxen helped move the sections and they were anchored on either side of the river, digging out a section of the bank and leveling it, much like fitting logs together to build a cabin. The result was a sturdy log bridge, they could cross any time to hunt across the river. The bridge would be a wonderful place to sit and catch fish in warm weather.

Since it was still spring, the men folks decided to at least plant a garden, fresh vegetables would be nice. Serious field planting would wait until next year. A trip to town for seeds, more tools, and another plow would be necessary. There were so many things they needed. Joseph decided this first trip to the acreage he was to inherit was really a fact-finding mission. Now he could make a list of all necessary things they needed, and they could visit his parents one more time.

Life is so uncertain, he wanted to sit across the table from his father, Israel, once more and ask his advice. Israel had always been a great storyteller and of sound and long memory. These traits would remain with most of the other family members. Just to describe the beauty of the river, the huge oaks, and the abundance of wild gooseberries and plums would give Israel a sense of his son's appreciation of his inheritance. Joseph looked forward to going back to visit and buying needed supplies before the frost of October.

Winter will be here, Dave said, "before you can skin a cat." Up before the sun, every morning the men of the family laid out the garden and worked on building what furniture they had to have. The women, with help from the children, got the wagons emptied and swept clean the house and cabin.

In late September of 1798, Joseph and Dave took the two wagons and made the long trip to Newberry for supplies. Sarah, Joseph's wife, had died from an unknown fever six weeks before the planned trip. By necessity, grief had to be short-lived when living in the back country far from civilization, no doctor or medical care. Joseph realized this and even though he loved his wife, he realized death comes to everyone and he knew he had to provide for his children. The trip could not be cancelled, and he so wanted to see his family in Newberry once more. Apparently, not only did Joseph bring back supplies from Newberry on this trip, but he also brought back a wife. Her name was Bathsheba.

The first three children listed below belonged to Joseph and his first wife. The others were the children of Joseph and Bathsheba Gauntt. Joseph had to be married more than once. There were twelve children, the two oldest brothers were the administrators of Joseph's estate in 1816 and Bathsheba who was mentioned as his widow had to sue the two brothers in court to receive her one third of Joseph's estate. After Joseph's death, Bathsheba married Benjamin Stubbs. I understand that. She was left with all those children, the youngest being three years old and needed help to provide for them. I find it hard to believe the two brothers would be so callus as to refuse their own mother her part of Joseph's estate. Therefore, I believe their mother was not Bathsheba.

The location of Joseph's inherited land being on the North Edisto river where Chinkepin Creek entered the North Edisto in present day Lexington County would have been near the little village of Steedman. The first bridge on the North Edisto after Chinkepin Creek flowed into the river is today at Steedman. The next bridge on the North Edisto is near the ancestral home of my family at Rayflin.

I have heard many times the stories my Uncle Leon Gantt told. One of these stories spoke of a log bridge across the North Edisto at Rayflin. The story told by my great granddaddy, Jacob Kelly 'Kell" Gantt, Leon's grandfather spoke of Russel Gunter crossing the log bridge spanning the North Edisto river to hunt squirrels. Russel killed a few and stuffed them in his cloth hunting bag. As he got almost to the log bridge, he could hear the howls of a pack of wolves; they could smell the blood of the squirrels in his bag. Grandaddy Kell Gantt also remembered so many passenger pigeons settling on pine saplings that the trees would bend over, almost touching the ground. Grandaddy Kell Gantt was born in 1854, just before the War Between the States. The land at Rayflin on the North Edisto river was the homeplace of Russell Gunter, grandfather of Kell's wife, Peninnah Woodward Gantt born 1860.

The land at Rayflin is described in legal records as the homestead of Russel Gunter, deceased. The land was passed from Russel to Peninnah and Jacob Kelly 'Kell' Gantt through Peninnah's Aunt, Merari Gunter Shaffer. "Auntie" as Merari was called was a sister to Peninnah's mother, Ara. Aunt Merari lived at Rayflin with Kell and Peninnah until her death in April 1910. Merari's husband, Charles Shaffer was killed in The War at the Battle of Boonsboro, Maryland in September 1862. Merari and Charlie had no children.

Children of Joseph and 1) Sarah (had to pick a name and the repetition of names being so relevant, it is Sarah in this interpretation) 2) Bathsheba Gauntt: (listed in the estate settlement). Estate administrators were his two eldest sons, Jacob, and Israel Gauntt.

1. Jacob Gauntt, born the 12th of June 1790, died in Elmore county town of Tallassee, Alabama in 1855, married Mary Gunter.
2. Israel Gauntt Sr., born the 4th of March 1791, had land holdings purchased in 1840, amounting to over 10,000 acres, land across the North Edisto, near Steedman. He is buried at a cemetery called Dry Branch about two miles from Steedman.
3. Walter Gauntt, born the 13th of April 1795, moved to Tallassee, Alabama. I have no further information on this son.
4. Elizabeth Gauntt, born the 11th of March 1797.

5. Eli Gauntt, born 12th of February 1799, all indications point to Eli being the original owner of the Gauntt Bible, his sons were Uriah H. Gantt Sr. and Zimri Gantt. Those sons probably lived in Sugar bottom, near the Gantt home at Rayflin. Uriah H. Sr. is buried there.

6. Elijah Gauntt, born 17th of July 1802 Elijah Gantt, (spelling of surname changed in this generation), Elijah Gantt married Elizabeth Gunter, daughter of Russell and Elizabeth Nelson Gunter, Elijah and Elizabeth are my third great grandparents and are buried at the John Gunter Mill Cemetery near Seivern , Aiken County SC. Aiken did not become a county until 1871, so I guess Elijah was born in Lexington County. I will talk more about Elijah Gantt.

7. Joseph Mooney Gauntt, born 1st of January 1804, moved to Tallassee, Alabama.

8. Elisha Gauntt, born 6th June 1805.

9. Hannah Gauntt, born 30th of September 1807.

10. John Gauntt, born 1st of November 1809.

11. Samuel Gauntt, born 18th of April 1811, died 1876, married Elizabeth Ann Lewis and is buried at Pine Grove Baptist Church. I will talk more about Samuel Gantt also, very familiar with this family.

12. Cary Gauntt, born 13th of December 1813.

Names of the children came from Joseph's Estate Settlement, the birthdates from the Bible of Uriah Hubbard

Gauntt Sr. born 1833, died 1898. Uriah H. Sr was the son of #5 above, Eli Gauntt. I did not see this Bible but was told it existed.

I am, however, familiar with Uriah Hubbard Gauntt Jr., grandson of Eli Gaunt, above called Mr. Hubbard by my family. Mr. Hubbard and his family lived within two miles from where I grew up, in a section of Lexington County, SC. called Sugar Bottom near the North Edisto River. I do remember seeing Mr. Hubbard's daughter, Attalee, several times. I was told my Grandfather, Ulysses Kelly Gantt called "Kelly" courted Miss Attalee at one time. Four of Joseph's children also stayed in Lexington District, after Israel was born in 1791, in Newberry County, he moved to Lexington District with his parents. Eli was born in 1799 in Lexington and spent his whole life there. Elijah born 1802 (my direct ancestor) and Samuel born 1811 also were born there and are buried there. Eli, Elijah, and Samuel spent their lives since birth in Lexington District. I have visited the graves of these four, Israel Sr, Eli, Elijah, and Samuel.

* * * * *

Israel Gantt Sr. #2, above, born 1791 died 1st June 1854, married Sarah Williams and lived on a large section of land across the North Edisto River from Steedman, South Carolina on land he acquired according to land records in Lexington District in 1840.

The children of Israel Sr. and Sarah Williams were:

1. Dr. Jacob Kelly Gantt married first Priscilla Veal and second Cassaline Gantt, daughter of Elijah and Elizabeth Gunter Gantt. Dr. Gantt's monument has not been discovered but is believed to be located on the slope above Goose Platter Creek in Aiken County. I have met several people who remember this cemetery, but the story is the land was cleared, even the cemetery was pushed up.
2. Elliot Gantt, married Ann E. Veal.
3. Drayton Gantt, married Caroline Steedman. Drayton fought in "The War", was wounded in the conflict, and made it to the home of his sister, Eleanor Gantt Jones, who lived in Oglethorpe, Georgia. Drayton died in Georgia, there is a monument near his sister, Eleanor, no dates, only the epitaph "Johnston's Army CSA".
4. Eleanor Gantt, married W.B. Jones, lived in Oglethorpe, Georgia and buried there.

I received this information in 1985, a lifetime ago, it seems.

Samuel Gantt #11 above, married Elizabeth Ann Lewis and was the ancestor of my stepmother Jeanette Gantt, so I am very connected to Samuel's family. I grew up knowing this family well. Granddaddy Frank Gantt, Jeanette's father, would visit us and we spent time with him and his wife, Grandmama Maggie. My daddy married Jeanette Gantt in 1962 and they became my family too.

What do I remember of Frank and Maggie? Grandma Maggie was the daughter of Almon Gunter and his wife Louisa, maiden name also was Gunter. She died in June 1978. I remember attending the service at Pine Grove Church with a sleeping baby on my lap, my youngest daughter, Paige. Grandma Maggie loved flowers and was a wonderful cook. Her iced tea was very strong and very sweet. Her appearance always neat, she was slender, with eyeglasses and short gray hair. Her eyes twinkled when she smiled, skin very tanned from spending hours in the sun tending her flowers. She always wore dresses, like most women at that time and age. They had an indoor bathroom, tub, sink, and commode. The tub was not used for bathing. Every time I was there the tub was full of Maggie's potted plants. She was a sweet lady, loved working in her yard, and cooking for her family.

The cement block house still stands, near Fairview Crossroads. Next door to the right was a garage covered in tin, Granddaddy Frank's mechanic shop. He worked for many years at the Holley Tractor Company in Aiken repairing tractors. He was a super smart man. He loved to broadcast over his CB radio and was, like my daddy, fond of bluegrass music. He was also a great storyteller, with a long memory, and a photographer, a craft inherited from his father, Joseph Gantt. In one of bedrooms hung a very large, framed picture of Granddaddy Frank's grandparents, Samuel and Elizabeth Lewis Gantt. Momma Jeanette inherited the large picture and gave it to me.

Children of Samuel and Elizabeth Lewis Gantt:

1. John Elmore Gantt, born 1837, died 1922, served

in the Confederate army, was injured at Frazier's Farm, and had his right arm amputated.

2. Samuel C. Gantt, born 1843, died 1927, served in the Confederate army and also loss an arm, amputated due to injury.

3. Hannah Gantt Gunter-Wells, born 1845, died 1920, married William E Wells, born 1838, died 1920, and Virgil Alexander Gunter, born 1845, died 1928. Miss Hannah was the midwife who delivered my Uncle Leon.

4. Bersheba Gantt Hall, born 30 June 1851, died 1897 (age 45), married John Brooks Hall, born 1855, died 1930 .

5. Elizabeth "Betsy" Ann Gantt Hall, born 1856, died 1931, married Henry Curtis Hall, born 1855, died 1935, they married 1874.

6. Joseph Gantt, born 1858, died 1922, married first Jane Hall Gantt, died October 13, 1893, giving birth to their son, William Gantt. I knew him as Mr. Bill (info from Charlie Gantt, son of Mr. Bill), married second Lydia Emma Gunter Gantt, born 1874, died 1926. Joseph was a photographer, took lots of pictures of local families. Joe's second wife, Emma, was the object of affection and girlfriend of Outlaw Emmanuel Williams.

7. Martha Ann Zelia Gantt, born 1859, died 1922.

8. Jacob A. Gantt, born 1863, died 1914. This Jacob married Ella Burgess, born 1865, died 1918.

Kathy G. Widener

Where the roots are deep, there is no reason to fear the wind.

"To forget one's ancestors is to be a brook
without a source, a tree without a root."

—Chinese Proverb

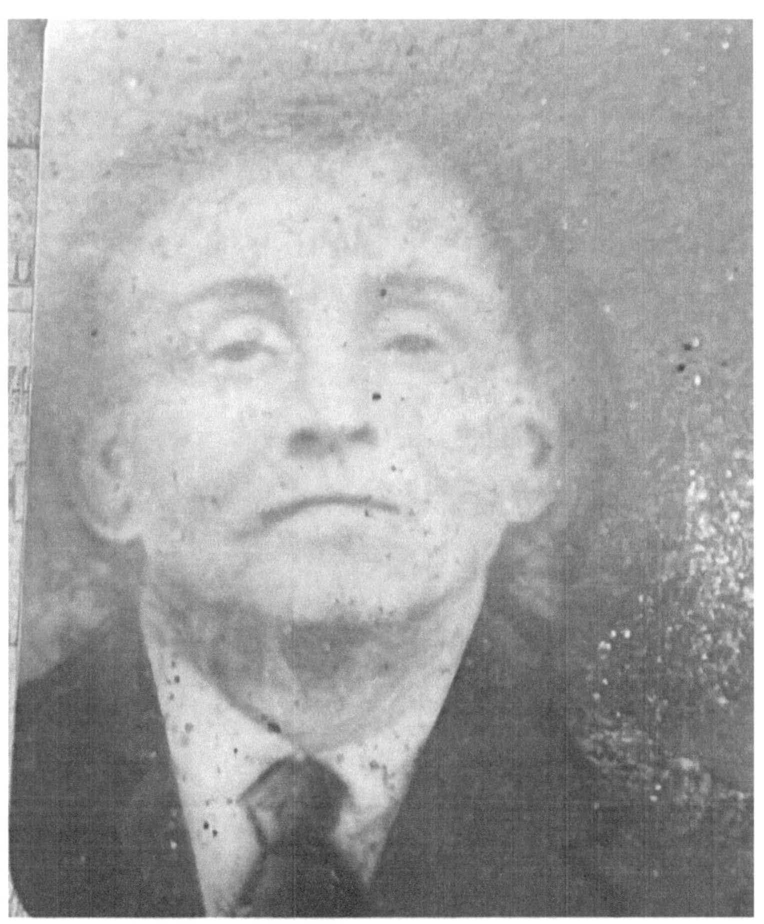

Samuel Gauntt, son of Joseph and Bathsheba

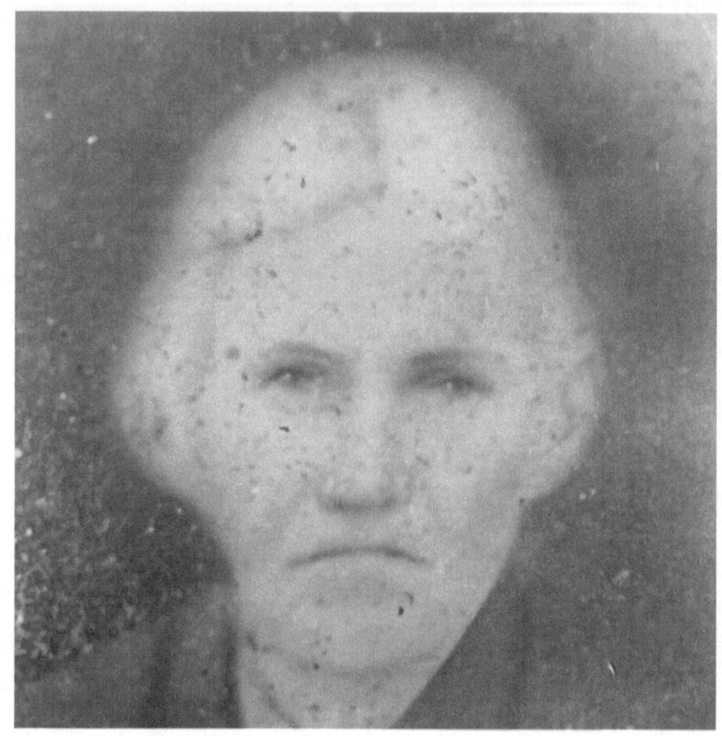

Elizabeth Ann Lewis

Frank and Maggie Gunter Gantt

Elijah Gauntt, son of Joseph and Bathsheba

Attalee Gantt, daughter of Uriah Hubbard Gantt

9. Elijah Gantt — An Outlaw in the Family

I have noticed not only are the names repetitive, but all the generations are names from the Bible, at least the first ten generations. There was not a Tom, Dick, or Harry in the bunch. That is a fascinating footnote to me. They surely were all religious and depended on a higher power, at least believers. I have always thought that way. No one is perfect, no not one. Elijah surely had at least one descendant who did not have a sterling character. His name was Emmanuel Williams, and his mother was Elijah's oldest child, Ninetta Gantt Williams.

I submit the following account about the bloody legacy of Emmanuel Williams. As the reader will conclude Emmanuel was an outlaw in the same sphere as Billy the Kid (1859-1881). They both were active in the late 19th century. Billy was more famous than Emmanuel and evidently brutally killed more people. Emmanuel (1865-1895) was a legend in the sandhills of South Carolina,

Aiken County (considered Lexington County at that time), and the area around Wagener and the little community of Seivern.

Growing up, I was told unimageable stories about Emmanuel Williams, first cousin of my Great Grandfather Jacob Kelly 'Kell' Gantt of Rayflin on the North Edisto River. An article, one source I refer to, was written by Daniel Harmon and published in the Saxe Gotha news in August 1980. Other sources include a newspaper from Opp, Alabama, about the history of the Gantt family, published 1973, but the best source is my Uncle Leon Gantt, the greatest storyteller I have ever known.

"Oscar J. Meyers, conductor for the Carolina Midland Railroad, sensed trouble as he looked along the aisle to the scarred mustachioed young man sitting alone, midway down the car. The man appeared sullen, but as the close seating quarters would allow, relaxed. Too relaxed Meyers thought, for he knew who the passenger was: Emmanuel Williams. In Edisto River environs, the name was widely recognized as a portent of danger."

The train was traveling through a lower Lexington County region covered with scrub oaks and pines in every direction. It was sand country; the train was attempting to navigate and was beginning to ascend a typical sandhill grade. The engineer was slowing ponderously as Meyers approached Williams for his fare.

Fare? The wiry passenger sneered and reached to his side holster. "Here's my fare," said Williams as he drew his gun.

Meyers was a big man, but quick and grabbed Williams hand on the way up. "You pay your fare or get off this train," Meyers replied angrily.

Williams reply was a curse, where upon Meyers yanked him up bodily and shoved him through the entry door and onto the stoop. The cars were by this time moving at a crawl up the incline. Without further negotiations, Meyers literally kicked the delinquent passenger off the train.

Williams stood up, brushing himself off. "Meyers, you are a dead man walking." In answer, Meyers threw Emmanuel's weapon into the trees slowly passing by. Meyers glanced back to see Emanuel trembling in rage as his figure receded from view.

Meyers was one of the few men who had ever tangled with Williams and lived. No one knows for sure where Emmanuel grew up, but his tombstone states his birth as May 13, 1865, the month after Lee's surrender at Appomattox. As far as we know, no other member of the family ran afoul of the law. He probably had a normal backcountry Reconstruction childhood.

The story was told to me many times of his exploits, by my Uncle Leon Gantt. His information came from his grandfather Jacob Kelly 'Kell" Gantt, who knew Emmanuel well as a first cousin and dealt with him on a regular basis when he was in the area. My uncle told me many things about Emmanuel, including the fact that his surname was not really Williams, it was Egans, his father was Jonathan Egans, of Indian blood. His mother, Ninetta, was riding home on horseback from Columbia the day he was born, stopped, and delivered her son, then continued on her way. That to me is hard to believe, but that is why some people become legends, for bad or good. That is the reason these improbable stories are remembered well over a hundred years after they occurred.

We are fairly sure he died a bachelor, but I have a copy of a tintype picture that was given to the mother of my step grandfather, Frank Gantt. Emanuel cared for Emma Gunter, who married Joseph Gantt, Frank's father, the result of their relationship; he wrote her a letter and sent her the picture. The copy is not great. Emmanuel definitely looks much older than thirty years. It also appears in this old photo that he has on handcuffs. I would not think a photo wearing handcuffs would appeal to most ladies, even a century ago. Maybe there was a point in sending her the photo. He was a boastful person and proud of his reputation. At the time of his death, Emmanuel Williams was, without a doubt, one of the most feared characters ever to roam the river land.

During the inquest after his death, Carolina Midlands Railroad Superintendent J.C. Keys testified that if Williams was feared to be in the vicinity. "I always feared for the safety of the railroad employees, property, and officials," Keys stated. "If he was reported seen in the area, I would leave a message for them, in hopes, they would be alert to danger." The message would have been sent by telegraph in the late nineteenth century.

Probably for good reason. Williams was openly suspected by the citizenry of countless crimes, ranging from making corn likker at a still, to train robbery, and murder. He was tried but acquitted of the slaying of an Aiken County clerk of court.

* * * * *

A local man, Wes Phillips, reported he was cleaning fish on the North Edisto when he heard a gunshot up near the railroad trestle about a hundred yards up the river. About fifteen minutes later, Emanuel walked into view in an apparently good mood. He stopped to chat with Phillips and offered him a swig from his bottle.

Emmanuel's mood changed when Phillips asked, "Did you hear a shot near the trestle about fifteen minutes ago?"

Emmanuel's replied. "Yeah, I did," he said with a scowl on his face. He then pointed his finger in Phillips face and said, "Wes, you didn't hear no gunshot and you ain't seen Emmanuel Williams today, understand!" The outlaw turned and walked away, confident that Phillips got his message.

The body of a local man was subsequently found near the trestle, shot in the head, his face covered in smut. The conclusion reached due to Emmanuel's later boasting that they, he and the victim, were planning to rob a local citizen who supposedly had money, they were rubbing black smut on each other's faces as a disguise, when his partner closed his eyes for Emmanuel to smut his face, he shot him. They apparently had a long-standing grudge between them and when his cohort closed his eyes, Emmanuel shot him and dispensed the grudge.

* * * * *

Williams was known to boast. There was a time he went

out West, with possibly less than honest intentions. Word eventually reached South Carolina that he had drowned in Alabama. But if folks breathed a collective sigh of relief, it was short lived. Williams soon returned in the flesh. He informed his friends of what had sparked the rumor he had started himself.

It seems he was involved in a train robbery which came to a climax as the train began a river crossing. The bandit found himself outnumbered and outgunned and was obliged to leap into the water. The train stopped. Guards and passengers debarked onto the trestlework's to take pot shots at the water bound robber. "They'd shoot and I'd dive," Williams recalled. He finally made good his escape, but his hunters, failing to see him surface a final time, wrote him off as deceased.

Though he was quite public with his tales, evidently local law enforcement was never sure if he was lying or telling the truth. He would brag, "I'll kill any man for five dollars," was especially goading to officers of the law. There were some locals who made a contract with him for his services, but only lost their money.

* * * * *

Much of the Wagener community turned out for an Independence Day barbeque picnic at Ready's pond. It was a pleasant day, beautiful location near the pond's head where a stream flowed under the dam. The weather was not sweltering, and a breeze made ripples on the pond. Everyone was looking forward to the food and camaraderie.

Williams was there, that was not unusual, since most of the attendees were friends or family members. The only problem was another desperado was also in attendance, possibly Charlie Weaver Jeffcoat, a known hothead in the community at the same period in time. Two hotheads with unstable minds could lead to trouble, and it did.

The pair early agreed to duel, but also agreed to wait until after the picknickers were fed, in order to actually be able to enjoy the barbeque without the bloody fight. Emmanuel even gave his opponent choice of weapons: guns, knives, or straight razors. The latter was chosen.

The men squared off at pondside, their left wrists were tied together with a ladies handkerchief and on signal began to butcher each other. A witness reported, "it was the goriest mess I've ever seen," which cannot be disputed, straight razors? At the end, Williams opponent just waved the razor towards his nemesis, so much blood in his eyes, he could not see. Finally, the victor, Williams severed the handkerchief and his opponent falling to his knees, a bloody pulp, was booted down to the water's edge, left to bleed to death. Standing over his opponent, Williams was heard to say, "I hate to kill a man like that, don't find a man that brave very often."

I heard the story about the Ready's pond picnic and Emanuel's fight from Uncle Leon. The above version was told to me exactly as it is written, right down to the two combatants having their left wrists tied together with a handkerchief.

* * * * *

Was there a speck of humanity in Emanuel? The only story I am aware of points to him caring for family, but in a strange way.

After the War Between the States, Emmanuel's uncle, Russel Ravenel Gantt moved to Covington County, Alabama. The following story unfolds on Christmas Eve day 1892…

Pickens Gantt and Jim Phillips had gone to Andalusia, Alabama to a bar room about 1:00 p.m. on that day and encountered Jim Barron, a Deputy Sheriff who was reportedly a friend of Pickens Gantt. Jim Barron, sitting on his horse, called to Pickens Gantt through the swinging saloon doors and said, "It's your set up." Pickens countered with, "You, Barron, are already drunk, and you do not need any more to drink".

Barron dismounted from his horse, walked into the bar where Pickens was standing, unholstered his pistol, and fired into Pickens's face, the bullet entering the cheek bone and upward into the brain. Pickens was removed to the home of a long-time friend, lived approximately two days, and passed away as a result of the bullet wound. When Jim Barron shot Pickens, he ran behind the counter of the bar, grabbed some money, jumped on his horse, and left Andalusia at a high rate of speed.

Jim Adkinson and George Duncan pursued him. He made a wide circle around the town then circled back to Sheriff Jim Bradshaw's office and gave himself up. He told the Sheriff he had killed the best friend he had. He was put under arrest and removed to Montgomery, Alabama for safe keeping. Two days later, he was returned to Andalusia for preliminary trial and placed in the Andalusia jail.

On December 27, 1892, Pickens Gantt was interred in the Gantt Cemetery at Gantt, Alabama. A group of men, including two Negroes, broke into the jail at Andalusia that night while the Sheriff was out of town and when the Sheriff returned Barron was dead. Apparently, a number of people were involved in Barron's demise, including a man by the name of Emmanuel Williams. Williams had a somewhat less than a good reputation according to sources living at the time. Pickens Gantt was a first cousin of Emmanuel's and he had traveled to Alabama with some of his cohorts for the express purpose of disposing of his cousin's killer, Jim Barron. He meant to avenge Pickens's death, then he disappeared.

* * * * *

In 1895, a succession of incidents was to conclude with a final brief showdown. Seivern at that time, 1895, was a bustling little town. Their main business was the Edisto Chalk Mine, the white chalk was more valuable than discolored strains in the surrounding terrain. The train at Seivern was at the end of the line, in a manner of speaking, there was a round house at Seivern, per my uncle, so the engine could be turned around and reverse directions.

The Carolina Midlands train would leave Wagener, the last major stop, late in the afternoon and steam on to Seivern about eight miles to the northwest. The engine would shut down at the Seivern station for the night and the crew, engineer, and conductor, would stay the night at the boarding house that stood on the Main street. There had been some trouble between Williams and Conductor Meyers three weeks before and the larger, quicker Meyers had embarrassed Williams once more. Meyers had wisely asked friends in Wagener and Seivern to alert him if Williams was in the vicinity. That fateful Friday night, October 11, 1895, the telegraph operator, C.W. Compton had sent a message to Wagener warning Meyers, "Keep your eyes open, something is wrong in town."

The brakeman, Henry Middleton, was accosted by Williams himself at gunpoint outside the boarding house that night. He asked Middleton some questions about the train and let him proceed inside. Williams turned and disappeared into the dark. Middleton carried mail and packages to be delivered to the boarding house, the center of activity in the little town. Middleton testified to that at the inquest into Williams' death.

Swinton Gunter, who ran the boarding house had already retired for the night, his wife awakened him and informed him there might be danger afoot. Gunter left his bed, glanced out the second story window of his private quarters, and froze in fright. He saw Williams walking down the street in the dim light. He dressed and hurried to warn his friend Meyers, not knowing Meyers had already received the message. Meanwhile, Meyers and Engineer Goodwin started towards the boarding house, Meyers carried a rifle.

Shortly after Gunter headed down the stairs, the crack

of a rifle shot was heard. At the inquest the next day, Compton, the telegraph operator, and Swinton Gunter were eyewitnesses. At the inquest, Meyers did not testify, and Gunter's testimony was very sketchy. The railroad ran a special train to get Meyers away from Seivern and any retaliation from Emanuel Williams' friends.

The whole incident was a mystery, and always will be. I myself heard from Uncle Leon that Emmanuel was shot in the back, that Swinton Gunter was the real killer, and that Emanuel had a wad of cash in his pants pocket that had mysteriously disappeared from his person.

Other tidbits about Emmanuel Williams: According to a notation in the Lexington Dispatch of 17th October 1894… Emmanuel Williams is a man 5 feet 8 inches in height, dark hair and eyes, dark complexion, and slight black moustache, most of the time he goes unshaven and dirty. Also, Uncle Leon told me, Sugar Bottom was not named because there was so much moonshine made in the area, as had been told, but was named by the Outlaw himself because there were so many pretty and sweet girls who resided there.

Evidently, according to my uncle, Emmanuel was also a trickster. A dance was being held with several area players strumming tunes on banjos and guitars, surely a jug or two. Emmanuel dosed the water buckets with croton oil, which among other side effects acts as a laxative. To add insult to injury, he greased all the door knots inside to make it difficult to open the doors in a hurry.

Emmanuel was a legendary outlaw, he killed at least a dozen men, robbed banks and trains out west. He was even reportedly to be a member of the Dalton gang when they attempted to rob two banks in one day in Coffeyville, Kansas. There were five members of the gang, Dick Broadwell, Bill Powers, and the three Dalton brothers that were killed by the citizenry that day, October 5, 1892. Many believe there was a sixth member who got away.

So many stories, fact is however stranger than fiction. Maybe Emmanuel did ride with the Dalton gang. He did most certainly leave a bloody legacy. Emmanuel Williams is buried in the John Gunter Mill Cemetery near Seivern South Carolina. The epitaph on his tombstone is inscribed, 'The weary are at rest'. Does this refer to Emmanuel Williams or to the citizens of the Edisto river area?

> "If you cannot get rid of a family skeleton,
> you may as well make it dance."
>
> —George Bernard Shaw

Emmanuel Williams, outlaw, and grandson of Elijah Gantt.

Pickens Gantt, son of Russell R. Gantt, lived in Alabama.

10. The Elijah Gantt Family

Elijah was born on the 17th of July in 1802. He married Elizabeth Gunter. The homeplace of Elijah and family is unknown, probably somewhere in the Sugar Bottom area of Lexington County, close to the black waters of North Edisto Place. I believe that, mainly because he married Russell and Elizabeth Nelson Gunter's oldest daughter and child. I know Russell's home was at Rayflin. That was so stated in a land record of the property, saying it was the 'homestead of Russell Gunter, deceased'.

In the 19th century, traveling was not easy. There were few choices, horse and buggy, mule, and wagon (which farm families leaned toward, as more efficient), walking, or taking the train. That points to the conclusion that his home was not too distant. I'm pretty sure Elijah couldn't have lived far from the Gunter home in Rayflin. I recently heard the homeplace of Elijah Gantt was indeed in the area of Sugar bottom, the Henry Lyles place. By necessity, the family of Elijah Gantt had to be up with the sun. There were a lot of mouths to feed in Elijah's family with thirteen children.

A grey dawn would peep above the thick forests and undergrowth to the east. Depending on the season, fires had to be stoked and grits and fatback prepared in an iron skillet on the wood cook stove. Lizzie, wife of Elijah, had to have her coffee, black and hot, no matter the temperature outside.

When breakfast was on the table, the children were called in to have their breakfast. Lizzie received few breaks from tending to children, cooking, cleaning, and washing clothes. The first twenty-six to thirty years of their married life, Lizzie had a child on her hip. Ninetta was the oldest, born on the 19th of January 1826. The last and youngest was Victoria Ann Ceris, born the 7th of February 1852. There were at least six boys, five of whom served in the Confederate Army. There may have been more. During the years Elijah and Lizzie raised their children, doctors were not easily available near home, midwives delivered most children, many did not survive. My Uncle Leon, Aunt Elsie, my Daddy, Robert, and my two sisters were delivered by midwives. My life and early childhood were similar to my family's in the nineteenth century.

Elijah and Lizzie farmed, the older boys, Caswell, Ravonell, and Uly helped with the plowing, tending their livestock, and butchering the animals for meat. The older girls, Ninetta, Zelia, and Elizabeth, helped their mother, Lizzie, with the cooking, cleaning, washing clothes by hand, and of course, canning their vegetables. In the spring and summer, vegetables from their garden were plentiful, but after the fall harvest, no more fresh vegetables except sweet potatoes, that could be banked (not sure what it means to bank sweet potatoes? Google it.) or collards, turnips, or mustard greens which are more prevalent in the cold temperatures of winter.

The Gantts and all country folks had to preserve what they could for leaner times. The information I got from my youth growing up in the country, greens aren't good until a good frost falls on them.

As the years went by, the younger kids grew and aged into helping more with the labors of planting and sowing the fields, scrubbing, and raking the sandy yards. The women had cast irons shaped with a point, something, like today's electric irons. When clothes were washed, the smoothing irons, as they were called, were propped up, the flat side towards the blazing fire. They had a wash day once a week, ironing to follow with the hot flat irons.

By necessity, the boys were taught how to handle firearms and shoot. They did a lot of hunting for wild game in the surrounding forests and supplied meat for their table. They also were taught how to handle livestock and ride horses and mules. Sometimes the boys would ride out into the deep woods, always two together for safety. All Southern men and boys knew how to shoot, clean weapons, and ride. Growing up, they had no idea how important that would become.

Living in the back country came with advantages and a whole lot of difficulties. If dry goods, baskets, furniture, or any tools were needed, you had to ride in a buggy or wagon for hours to get to the nearest town or you had to make it yourself. Once you got to town, there was always a general store, probably more than one, where cloth for sewing clothing, pantry necessities like salt, flour, and baking soda could be purchased.

At home in the country, the air was clean and sweet smelling, the sky above was blue with fluffy cotton clouds or at night a heaven full of bright shining stars. The quiet of a country night has no comparison to living in town. In the country you can actually be surrounded by quiet, except for the night birds and the chirping of crickets.

Elijah and Elizabeth "Lizzie" Gantt were blessed by God above in at least one big way. All their children, at least the ones I know about, outlived their parents, except one, Israel Henephen Gantt. He died early in the 'The War'.

Elijah Gantt was born the 17th of July in 1802 and died 22nd of April 1876. His wife, Elizabeth 'Lizzie' Gunter Gantt, was born the 4th of May 1806 and died 28th of November 1886. Lizzie testified to a court in support of her mother receiving a pension after her father had passed away. Russell Gunter was a veteran of the War of 1812, and Elizabeth stated her birth and said she could remember when her father returned home from the fight against Great Britain. That was after her father died at age 98.

Lizzie's mother applied for the pension at age 95 and needed witnesses to attest to her age, even though she had a family Bible. Attached to her application to receive a pension were page after page of witnesses that attested to the fact that Elizabeth and Russell Gunter lived as man and wife. she needed the pension to comfort her in her aged and infirm condition. These old folks were tough!

I am fortunate, I have a photo of my third great grandfather, Elijah Gantt.

Children of Elijah and Elizabeth 'Lizzie' Gunter Gantt:

1. Ninetta Gantt born the 19th of January 1826, died 21st of May 1910 (mother of the outlaw, Williams).
2. Russell Ravonell Gantt born the 5th of September 1828, died 27th of September 1899 in Covington County, Alabama. Ravonell moved there after 'The War'.
3. Zelia Gantt born the 5th of March 1830, died 2nd of March 1920.
4. Ulyses 'Uly' Gantt born the 1st of December 1831, died 22nd September 1897.
5. Elizabeth Gantt was born on the 8th of November 1835.
6. Teresa 'Tessie' Gantt was born in 1838.
7. Cassaline Gantt born the 8th of October 1839, died 22nd April 1918.
8. Caswell Gantt born 1840, died in Covington County Alabama.
9. Israel Henephen Gantt born 1842, died in the early part of the 'The War'.
10. Dorothy 'Dolly' Gantt was born on the 2nd of April 1844.
11. Elijah Monroe Gantt was born on the 13th of June 1846.
12. William Adolphus Gantt born 8th of March 1849, died 22nd of January 1898
13. Victoria Ann Ceris Gantt born 7th of February 1852, died 13th of February 1933.

Elijah Monroe Gantt, son of Elijah Gantt, Confederate soldier.

11. 'The War' Sons of Elijah

Every born Southerner I grew up with during the 1950's and 1960's knows what those two words refer to. It is of course the War Between the States or Civil War. I have no intentions of rehashing the war fought between the North and South from the beginning in 1861 until the final shot and surrender in April 1865 at Appomattox Courthouse, Virginia. I have visited all major battle sites and am well aware of the bloodshed and carnage that took place.

My intentions are only to honor the memory of Elijah and Lizzie Gantt's sons that fought in that awful war. The reported casualties, both North and South, is believed to be about 655,000 military, contrast that with the military casualties in WWII 405,400. Of course, there are many ways to look at the numbers, one has to consider population percentages and of course the total killed and injured of the civilian population. I would say 655,000 thousand is a whole heap of "cannon fodder".

When I was a college student in the mid 1980's, I took a class called Southern Studies. There is a school of thought called the Magnolia School. In southern studies, we discussed the thought that out of the southern defeat of the South emerged the "lost cause" and the glorification of the prewar South. Writers wrote about it and the Southerners were supposedly overwhelmed by what a wonderful glorious antebellum South was destroyed by those meddling Yankees.

I submit that the sons of Elijah and Lizzie had no such thoughts. We're talking 'salt of the earth people.' They were farmers, worked daylight to dusk. They saw the War as a duty to defend the South. They definitely were not as rich as the antebellum class depicted in *Gone With The Wind* by Margaret Mitchell. The book was phenomenal, the only book Miss Mitchell wrote, but she only needed that one.

"There was a land of Cavaliers and Cotton Fields called the Old South. Here in this pretty world, Gallantry took its last bow. Here was the last ever to be seen of Knights and their Ladies Fair, of Masters and of Slave. Look for it only in books, for it is no more than a dream remembered, a Civilization gone with the wind," this was a quote authored by Ben Hecht, a writer of screen plays and more than thirty-five books. I always thought Miss Mitchell herself wrote this quote. I absolutely loved Miss Mitchell's book, but my family never had the money, land, or slaves of Tara. I have read *Gone With The Wind* three times; the book is much better than the movie. I have seen the movie only once on the big screen, in 1968. Jimmy took me, tickets cost two dollars apiece, and I still have the ticket stubs in a scrapbook.

Before I discuss the Confederate soldiers in my Gantt

family, I would like to give the reader an insight into what connection I myself had with slavery that occurred in the South, a true story.

My husband's father worked exclusively for big farmers as an overseer. The Wideners lived at one time on the farm of Mr. Charles Venning. Mr. Venning owned many acres in Montmorenci and had black and white workers. All workers for the Venning family were paid a wage, they were treated well by the overseer, my father-in-law. Jimmy took me over to visit the Venning family farm shortly after we started dating in 1966.

There was a long sandy drive leading to the overseer's house from the paved road. Directly across from the overseer's house was a big two story, unpainted house called the Wells place. That old house was the home of Mattie, Pap, and Mattie's mother. The house was there during 'the War'. Sitting on the porch that day was an old black lady, waving a fan to stir a breath of cool breeze. Jimmy knew her, I think he called her Aunt Janie.

He told me this black lady sitting beside the door on the porch was born a slave and she told him when they lived in the overseer's place in the late 1950's she could remember when the boys came home from the war. They were all wearing those red union suits, what we called long-handled underwear. He used to walk over and talk to her. Her eyesight was really bad when his family lived there, but he couldn't sneak up on her, she could tell it was him. Before Aunt Janie died, she had those cloudy cataracts removed and her vision was much better.

Russell Ravonell Gantt, son of Lizzie and Elijah, joined

the Confederate Army at Charleston on 12th April of 1862. He was assigned to Company I, South Carolina Infantry, enlisted by Captain Millhouse. Ravonell was crippled on James Island and spent the summer at home. In the fall, crops harvested, he rejoined his company in Virginia. He fought at Kingston, North Carolina, and was also present at the siege of Petersburg, Virginia, at Cold Harbor and in minor skirmishes. He was wounded in the head at Bermuda Hundred and for fifteen days his life hung in the balance, but he pulled through to fight another day.

In July he was wounded in the explosion at Petersburg, referred to as the Battle of the crater, when a mini ball struck his forehead. In June of 1863, his brigade under General Evans was sent to reinforce General Pemberton at Vicksburg, but reached there just before the city fell, and retreated to Jackson, Mississippi. He fought there and afterwards returned to Georgia and then to Charleston. He spent the winter on Sullivan's Island cutting wood for fires and building shelters for the Quarter Master Dept.

On his official record, 24th February through the 29th of February 1864, the nature of his service on Sullivan's Island is stated as a carpenter. Ravonell lived through the War, came home, and in 1872, moved with his family to Covington County, Alabama. From information I have, Ravonell killed some Yankees during Reconstruction and had to flee out of state to escape retribution. Reconstruction was the period after the War when the government was completely under Union control, it lasted until 1877.

Israel Henephen Gantt, son of Elijah and Lizzie, joined the Confederate Army 8th of April 1862 at Ridgeville,

South Carolina. He was a private in company K South Carolina Infantry. Israel H. Gantt contracted typhoid fever and died in a hospital near Germantown, Virginia, the 25th of August 1862. That is all that is available on his war record. I have seen a little song book where Israel H. wrote his name on the cover page, actually the little book was the big clue to what the H stood for, Henephen. That's one middle name I surely could not have guessed if I had not seen it in his own handwriting.

Elijah Monroe Gantt, son of Elijah and Lizzie, joined the Confederate Army on 28th of February 1863, assigned to Captain Elbert Gunter's 20th South Carolina Company. He mustered at Sand Dam near Wagener, South Carolina. He was paroled at Bennett House near Durham, North Carolina, 18th May 1865. I have Elijah M. Gantt's war record and pension record. I do not know where he fought but have interviewed several of his grandchildren over the years. I have copies of two pictures of him in his confederate uniform. I know much more about his life after the war.

He was a brother to my 2nd great grandfather, Ulysses S. Gantt. After the war, he moved to Springfield, South Carolina. He must have been a brilliant man. I have pictures from his granddaughters Juanita Sligh and Marvis Smith. From all the information I have on Elijah M. Gantt, he was a carpenter, built a huge wood clapboard house in Springfield, also a photographer. He developed the film in a small dark room off the back porch. He had negatives on glass used as windowpanes in his house in Springfield, SC. I also have pictures of him with his wife, Henrietta Phillips, and their entire family. I even have an original picture of Elijah Monroe, sitting in a ladder back chair in someone's yard.

I believe my Uncle Leon, the memory specialist of my childhood, told me the picture was taken at Rayflin at great granddaddy Jacob Kelly 'Kell' Gantt's house. Highly probable, Kell was Elijah Monroe's nephew. When I visited Elijah M's granddaughter, Juanita Sligh, in Columbia, not only did she share pictures of him and his family, she shared a handwritten description of what Elijah M. and most other confederates soldiers did to survive after the War.

It was written in his own hand as follows: "There was nothing in the country to do to make money, I made tubs, pails, and barrels out of juniper for farmers to fill, agreed to fill them myself with peas, corn, and beans. I worked on plows, wagons, made plow stocks, axe handles, and saddles. I also mended bridles, harness, and made shoes, boots, and did all kind of shop work, cut, and hauled timber, rafted it down the North Edisto to Charleston, and got the pitiful sum of 8 dollars. I installed machinery that ran the sawmills to cut timber into lumber. I worked in Columbia with one of my cousins for $20 per month and bread and meat. During Reconstruction, I was all this time in a military company to keep the carpet baggers from finally getting the state all together under Negro rule. This was at Sand Dam, Lexington county, South Carolina. We had about 40 men, most all good old confederate soldiers.

"About this time there was a threatening of a negro uprising. So, we assembled at our rendezvous and stayed under arms all day with picket lines to Batesburg with cousins from Convent Church. We assembled, ready to go at a minute's warning". A description of Elijah Monroe from one of his granddaughters: E.M. Gantt was about 5 feet tall, had a long beard, weighed about 130 pounds, his wife, Henrietta was about 6 feet tall, weighed about 220 pounds. He lived at Sand Dam in Lexington County, highway 113 between Wagener and Fairview, river bridge, then moved to Springfield, South Carolina. Also, he was described as being very slow, but thorough at any task he undertook.

William Adolphus Gantt, born the 8th of March 1849 and died 22nd of January 1898. Adolphus married Mary Adella Phillips, sister of Henrietta Phillips, who married Elijah Monroe Gantt. Again, we have brothers married to sisters. I have a photo of the youngest son of Uncle Adolphus, Jacob Ravenell called J.R. One of the sweetest ladies in my church was J.R.'s daughter, Della Kyzer. She also was one of the leaders of my girl scout troop. Miss Della and my Daddy, Robert Gantt, went to school together, at Fairview, near Wagener, SC. Adolphus, and Elijah Monroe, were both members of the Gunter Company and joined near sand dam between Fairview and Wagener.

Uncle Adolphus visited his nephew, Kell Gantt at Rayflin after the war, walking across Kell's pasture a horned sheep ram, butted him several times. The ram would walk away and then run at Adolphus; head lowered. Adolphus got tired of this play, "I'll fix you," he said, as he pulled a knife from his overall pocket. The next time the ram hit him, almost knocking him again to the ground, Adolphus buried the knife in the ram's neck and the animal staggered away. This too was a Leon Gantt story.

Caswell Gantt was born in 1840, and married Mary A. Williamson in 1860. His family moved after 'the War' to Covington County, Alabama. That is where he died. I do not have a copy of his war record, but I know he served. In the late 1970's, before the Confederate Relic Room was moved to the State Museum, it was located diagonally across from the SC State Archives on Sumter St. in Columbia. My sister with her daughter, Scarlett, myself with my two young children, Melanie and Jason, visited the Confederate Relic Room. There was a Confederate Military display case. Behind the glass on the red velvet background were musket balls, pistols, and long guns, one was a Confederate musket labeled "belonged to Caswell Gantt of Wagener, SC and carried during the War."

Ulysses Serenas Gantt 'Uly" was born 1st December 1831, married Martha Matilda Cook, died at his Black Creek home in between Fairview and Pelion 22nd of September 1897. Uly was my 2nd great grandfather. Grandpa Uly joined the Confederate Army at Camp Hampton near Columbia, SC on 3rd of January 1862. The next muster found Private Ulysses S. Gantt at Camp Wappo near Charleston. He served in the 19th Regiment, Company K. The regiment left camp Wappo on 11th March 1862 and arrived in Corinth, Mississippi just in time to engage Union Commander, Major General Henry W. Halleck as the Union forces besieged the vital southern town beginning on 29th April 1862.

The town was captured by the Union after a month-long siege, the rail lines here led to the Confederate heartland as well as to the seacoast. By November of 1862, Uly and his regiment were in Murfreesboro, Tennessee. The new year, 1863, found Uly's company and the brigade his company belonged to on picket duty six miles from Shelbyville, Tennessee on the Triune Road. They stayed near Shelbyville through August 1863. The muster report shows their duty station as Tyners and notes their retreat from Tullahoma, Tennessee on the night of the 30th of June and reached Chattanooga on the 6th of July 1863.

By September 1863, Uly's regiment was on Missionary Ridge in the battle of Chickamauga. This was a major battle, the Union (Army of the Cumberland) faced the Confederate (Army of Tennessee). Where did this information come from? I did not make this up. The Company K 19th Regiment had a dedicated company clerk, T. Cary. This man wrote an account of every muster (two months) and it matches the war record of Uly. I am quoting T. Cary, "The company changed positions frequently during the month of September and on the 20th was engaged in the Battle of Chickamauga, had one enlisted killed and six wounded, one of whom has died since. On 23rd September, changed position to Missionary Ridge. November & December 1863, Dalton, Georgia.

"This company was engaged on picket duty in front of Chattanooga until the 25th day of November, and on that day the enemy attacked us. After a desperate engagement, our forces were repulsed. This company lost four men missing, supposed to be taken prisoners of the enemy. We commenced the retreat on the night of the 25th of November and reached Dalton, Ga, on the 27th Nov 63, where we are now."

I copied this company report many years ago. Thanks to T. Cary, his report was written almost 160 years ago. Grandpa Uly did survive the War, his company was reported near Dalton, Georgia until the 1st of April 1864. When they finally moved on, the company headed South. Ulysses S. Gantt was, however, taken prisoner outside of Atlanta on the 22nd of July 1864, spent time in a prison camp in Camp Chase, Ohio. On the 6th of June 1865, he was released by order of the President. That order came from President Andrew Johnson. How long did it take for Grandpa Uly to get home? No one knows, he might have been able to ride a train, but there is a good chance, he had to walk most of the way from the POW camp in Ohio to Lexington County, SC.

* * * * *

During the War, my great grandma, Peninnah Woodward Gantt was a small child. She was born the 10th of May 1860 and lived at Rayflin during the War with her grandparents, Russell and Elizabeth Gunter and her mother, Ara Woodward. Ara had died in May of 1864. Russell knew the Yankees would be paying them a visit on Sherman's March to the Sea. The news had been received by telegraph and neighbors spread the warning. Ara would not be present to comfort the little girl, her death precluded the Yankees' arrival, and her father was away soldiering, as her mother had explained to Peninnah. The blue clad soldiers arrived just as expected. It would have been a traumatic experience for a small child to see her home invaded by strangers in blue, ransacking everything, searching through drawers, closets, flipping the mattresses on beds, looking for anything of value and absconding with any food the family had in the kitchen pantry and the smokehouse.

The soldiers did not hurt the little girl, some even tried to reassure her everything would be fine. But there were always a few that were not kind. There was an old, almost blind man, his back bent to the extent he could not stand straight living in the house at Rayflin when the Yankee soldiers arrived. Uncle Leon said his name was Uncle Ben Gunter, and some of the soldiers got great glee, slamming the door on his bony, fragile fingers. Old Ben could have been a brother to Russell.

Both of Peninnah's grandparents were there but, nearing advanced age themselves, they did not know how to comfort a child in these circumstances. They certainly knew they could not stop the attack without risking worse retaliation.

A few soldiers invaded the yard, chasing down their chickens and carrying them off across their saddles, the same with the three piglets in a pen up near the barn. The old sow, too big to carry, a Yankee soldier just shot her with his musket. They asked about livestock over and over, they especially wanted horses and mules. A black man, named Cheeseman, had taken the Gunter's three horses and two mules deep in the river swamp. As soon as the folks at Rayflin heard that one of General Sherman's columns was advancing toward their area, Russell sent Cheeseman, with food and provisions to camp out of sight in the swamp and protect the livestock from being stolen. He also handed him a musket, gun powder, and lead balls.

He told Cheeseman he might need protection too, we're talking deep in the river swamp, a place where a lot of dangerous creatures lived. Russell had enough trust and faith in Cheeseman that he sent a weapon along with him and the livestock. Cheeseman was probably a slave of the family, but he and the other black folks that lived at Rayflin protected the family the best they could and refused to tell the soldiers where their stock could be found.

Finally, after harassing the family about where their livestock might be with no positive result, the soldiers mounted their horses and headed towards the north. But, not before piling dry branches up next to an outside pillar under the side porch. They then set the stacked limbs on fire in an attempt to burn the Gunter home. Luckily for the family, the Yankees were in a big hurry to raid the next farm. They did not tarry even a few minutes longer to assure their evil intention was successful.

One of the menfolk present acted quickly, raked the burning pile from under the house, and dumped a full water bucket on the blaze. Fortune smiled on them that day. As bad as the experience was, the black folk were loyal to their family. They all were calm throughout the scary attack and there was a full water bucket sitting on the porch in easy reach. After the fire was extinguished, the whole group bowed their heads and Russell said a prayer of thanks that they were all safe. Attacked and frightened, but not defeated. This story was told to me by Leon Gantt.

Another story I heard shows how the Union soldiers were foiled in their attempt to destroy a South Carolina lady's home and save her and the children from ruin. The lady, Mrs. Bentley, was left alone, her husband and every man in the neighborhood was away fighting except for a couple of black men, slaves, that she trusted with her home and her life. She came up with an ingenious plan. Hearing the Yankees would arrive in a few days, she sent the two black men into the surrounding forest with instructions to kill a deer. When they returned with the carcass, she told them to hang the animal beside the stairs, but it should be out of sight from any windows and the front door.

In the hot and muggy heat of the South, it didn't take long for the dead animal to become putrid and stink to high heaven. The lady had an extreme allergic reaction to strawberries. If she ate just a few, she would break out in red, angry whelps all over her body. When she heard shooting and shouting from the house of her neighbor two miles away, she knew the Union soldiers were rampaging close at hand and she knew they would soon be riding up her sandy driveway. She poured herself a glass of water and opened a large jar of strawberry preserves. Grabbing a spoon, she sat at the table and consumed at least half of the jar of preserves. Almost immediately the whelps appeared, beginning to sting and itch on her chest, face, and down her arms. She was miserable but it was part of her plan.

Within a few minutes, she heard the hoofbeats entering the drive. It was late evening and there were two kerosene lamps in the entry way. The horses came to an abrupt stop at the base of the front steps as the lady stepped on the porch. The commander of the soldiers began to speak, the lady interrupted him saying, "We are sick in this house, please go." There she stood, covered in red whelps, the smell of death hanging in the air. The commander looked at her and turned his gaze to his followers. He saw the fright in their eyes and the shock on their faces looking at the woman standing on the porch, disheveled appearance and angry rash covering her body. "I am sorry we interrupted your evening, ma'am. I do hope you will recover." Then they all turned their mounts and fled back down the driveway.

History is so fascinating! At the beginning of the 'War', Wilmer McLean owned a farm in Virginia near a creek called Manassas. Actually, that creek flowed through Mr. McLean's farm. The very 1st Battle, Manassas, was fought on his farm. After the Battle took place on his farm, cannons firing, soldiers taking cover in his barn and trampling his fields, his home peppered by mini balls; a cannon ball actually pierced through the house and landed in the kitchen fireplace. Mr. Maclean decided to move his family far from the forefront of the fighting.

Well, history can be unbelievable, Mr. McLean moved to Appomattox Courthouse, Virginia. If you are a history buff, you know the War ended in Mr. McLean's parlor, with the surrender of General Lee to General Grant. His property was of course destroyed once again. His land was trampled by the soldiers in both armies, and the furniture in his parlor was stolen, seems everyone of rank in attendance wanted a piece of history. Fact is again stranger than fiction.

Another tale showcasing the South's stubborn resolve and long memory. Vicksburg, Mississippi, fell after a long siege (47 days) by the Union Army led by General U.S. Grant. The citizens of Vicksburg were starving, homes destroyed, and citizens killed. Before the Union succeeded, the people of Vicksburg were living in caves near the river. Finally, the Confederate forces had to capitulate on July 4th, 1863. The citizens of Vicksburg refused to celebrate July 4th Independence Day for seventy years. The generation of Vicksburg folks who experienced that awful siege, the starvation of their loved ones, the destruction of their once beautiful city, was a bitter memory. Most of the generation that were actually there had to pass away before the city participated in the celebration of Independence Day once again.

Interesting fact, battles had different names for Union and Confederate. The South named battles after the nearest town, the North named battles after the nearest river or creek. Think Antietam (North) Sharpsburg (South) same battle, Bull Run (North) Manassas (South) same battle, and Pittsburg Landing (North) Shiloh (South). This was not a strict rule. Gettysburg and Fredericksburg being two exceptions that come to mind, perhaps because the towns were where the fighting took place, not at some wilderness crossroads, but where the population lived. In Fredericksburg, it was house to house, urban warfare. The civilian population was involved in the battle.

General Robert E. Lee, Confederate General was pardoned by President Lincoln at Appomattox with the surrender of his Army in April 1864. But that was lost to history when Lincoln was killed just five days after Appomattox. In 1975, President Gerald R. Ford posthumously officially pardoned Lee using Lee's desk from Arlington House and restored his citizenship.

I had the honor of meeting Mrs. Ann Carter Zimmer, great granddaughter of General Lee when she came to speak at our Lee-Jackson Banquet in 2000. Mrs. Zimmer was living in Ohio at the time and had friends in the Ohio State University gourmet group. Mrs. Zimmer asked the group if they would be interested in rewriting and testing recipes of her great grandmother, Mary Custis Lee. She was surprised by those who clamored to help. Mrs. Zimmer had a copy of the notebook to use with the group but actually the Historical Society of Virginia let Mrs. Zimmer go through the original tattered notebook to read and review which recipes to convert.

Not only were there recipes for preparing food, but also remedies for treating medical conditions and how to prepare the best homemade cleaning solutions. They went through Mrs. Lee's tattered notebook of recipes, rewrote and tested them to appeal to modern cooks. The result was her book, *The Robert E. Lee Family Cooking and Housekeeping Book*. It is fascinating, lots of information on the family of General Lee, pictures, and of course the recipes. It is more a true story by a person who lived it than a cookbook. Mrs. Zimmer wrote a personal note and signed my copy.

"Time is a circus, always packing
up and moving away."

—Ben Hecht

Russell Ravenel Gantt, son of Elijah, Confederate soldier.

Elijah Monroe, son of Elijah in his Confederate uniform.

*In background The Wells House, standing during the
'War' forefront cousins of author's husband.*

12. Daughters of Elijah

The daughters of Elijah are historically as fascinating as his sons. The women, daughters of Elijah and Lizzie, went through just as many hardships as their brothers. They didn't go to War like the men, their brothers, and husbands. They didn't fight bloody battles and witness the horrors of the aftermath of those battles, dead bodies of soldiers on both sides tossed about like discarded trash, covered in blood.

They experienced the War and devastation on the Homefront. Some of Elijah and Lizzie's daughters had children of their own when the War came. It was not easy to feed and clothe their children without their menfolk present. These daughters had to look into the hollow eyes of their children, underfed and undernourished. They had to depend on their extended family for food. They lived isolated, with no transportation except by wagon that had to be hitched with collar, bit and bridle, long reins attached, the ends wrapped around the board used as a seat. Just hooking up the animal to the wagon was quite a chore, especially with small children clinging to their mother's skirts.

Only the youngest of the girls, Tirza, Cassaline and Ceris still lived with Lizzie and Elijah. They continued to help Lizzie with the cooking and cleaning. But in the end, those with the same family roots, kinfolks, were willing to help so that the children would be fed and cared for. Their sisters, Ninetta Gantt Williams, Zelia Gantt Gunter, and Elizabeth Gantt Altman all had small children, and all struggled to make ends meet. They farmed the land they lived on, cleaned, and cooked for their children, no men to help. They were all tough dedicated mothers. Sometimes Cassaline and Ceris would visit their sisters to help out, always bringing some meat and vegetables from their mother and father's larder.

How did Elijah's daughters live? We know most of his sons went away to fight the 'War' then came home to their farms and the devastation and reconstruction of the region in the aftermath, but what was their lives like, the menfolk away and children to feed.

1.) My readers have already heard the story of Uly Gantt's older sister, Ninetta, mostly remembered for being the mother of the outlaw Emmanuel Williams. Ninetta was married to Madison Williams. She did have four other children, one a daughter, Angeline Williams rests in the John Gunter Mill cemetery with her mother, Ninetta and her brother, Emmanuel. The other three were Jacob Colwell Williams, born 1855, James Madison Williams Jr., born 1857, who moved to Alabama, and Phoebe Alice, born 1861. Emmanuel took his mother's last name of Williams, even though he was reportedly an Egans. I would say his real father had no contact with him, did not know he was the father, or did not want to claim that right.

2.) Zelia Gantt was born in 1830 and married Elvin Gunter. She and Elvin had nine children, the youngest being Lydia Emma, born 1874, the girlfriend of the outlaw Emmanuel Williams, the same Lydia who married Joe Gantt, second son of Samuel, son of Joseph Gantt from Newberry. Emmanuel we already know is the son of Ninetta Gantt, daughter of Elijah. I feel like I am spinning around in circles or like a dog chasing his tail. They're all related to each other. Yes, it is no longer in doubt, I am my own cousin! Elvin, her husband, did live through the War, Zelia and Elvin had two daughters, Catherine Elizabeth born in 1863 and Alma born in 1864. After the end of the War and the birth of their youngest daughter, Lydia Emma, in 1874, Elvin abandoned his family, disappeared, and no one heard from him again. Zelia had a bit of land, about five acres, with an old farmhouse and a ramshackle barn. She, with her brood of children, would have starved if it had not been for her parents and other kin. Family had to stick together to survive.

Lizzie, Zelia's daughter, I can remember her myself, lived with her son, Ted Gunter. Miss Lizzie, who lived until 1962, and Ted lived across the river from Rayflin. Ted was a loner and a strange character, to say the least. But he was amazing at working on watches, taking them apart and replacing the little cogs and wheels. I was told by Uncle Leon that Ted made all their copper liquor stills in the 1920's and 30's. The stills were so perfect they were considered almost a work of art. I would pass Ted many times with his companion, a dog named Pup. As we passed, Ted would stop, turn, and watch our car until I was out of sight. Ted passed away in 1985 and my brother, Steve, made his coffin, that carpenter gene again.

3.) Elizabeth "Bathsheba" Gantt, born 1835, married Solomon Altman, born 1829, both interred in a cemetery in Batesburg. I'm thinking, how refreshing, a different surname for one of Elijah Gantt's daughters. Alas, that is short lived. Lizzie and Solomon had two children before he left for the "War" and four born afterward. I have no information as to where their homeplace was, I have been told that the Soloman Altman family homeplace was near the site of the Revolutionary War battle, Hell's Hole Creek, mentioned earlier. If so, that would be near the Batesburg-Leesville area. Elizabeth and Solomon Altman are buried at a family cemetery in Batesburg.

4.) Dorothy "Dolly" Gantt, born 1844, married James "Jack" Manderville Altman at her father, Elijah's, home on the 21st of January 1864. One of Dolly and Jack Altman's daughters, Eva Altman Strange, was born in 1883 and died in 1922. Fortunately, Eva Altman had a picture of her Gantt grandfather who was, of course, Elijah Gantt. It was an old tintype, but her granddaughter, Miriam Mitchell, copied it for me. That's how I came to possess a photograph of my third great grandfather, Elijah Gantt.

5.) Tirza Gantt, daughter of Elijah, never married. She was called "Tessie". She had a child born in 1862, don't know who the father was, but Tessie died young and the child, Rosa Lee, was abandoned.

That leaves two of Elijah's daughters, Cassaline, born the 8th of October 1839, and Victoria Ann Ceris Gantt, born on the 7th of February 1852.

6.) Cassaline Gantt, daughter of Elijah, I remember many talks with my uncle about Aunt Cassaline. She is buried at the John Gunter Mill cemetery. Her tombstone always mystified me. On her tombstone is stated: "Erected by Viola -Max-Grace and Robert Sternenberg" Who were the Sternenbergs? I went to my Uncle Leon for explanation.

Aunt Cassaline adopted the child, Rosa Lee, abandoned after her sister Tirza's death. I have a copy of a letter written to Miriam Mitchell (distant kin and fellow genealogist). She sent me the copy of a letter written by Mrs. Ming of Destin, Florida. Mrs. Ming was the child of Viola Sterenenberg Fulmer, and it gives much insight into Aunt Cassaline and her life. I will quote the interesting parts of Mrs. Ming letter, written in 1971. "I am Viola Sternenberg Fulmer's only child. Viola was Rosa Lee Gantt Sternenberg's child. The four children of Rosa Lee erected the tombstone on Cassaline Gantt's grave. From the info I received from my mother, Viola, they knew her as "Auntie". I do have from grandmother's possessions some letters written in the 1800's. I do not recall ever hearing how Grandmother and Grandaddy Sternenberg (Max) met. He was the son of a Sternenberg who sent his family to America from Germany to escape 'Kaiser Bill's' reign of terror. I have been told his father was one of the King's barons. Where the family settled here and how many of them there were, I do not know, but Grandmother and

Grandaddy lived in Giddings, Texas until Grandaddy died there on September 15, 1897 and was buried there. He was in the hardware and lumber business in Texas, also dealt in cotton futures, making huge amounts of money at times, and then losing the same way.

"My mother (Viola) has told me of her mother (Rosa Lee) putting her in the middle of their bed and letting her play with buckets of money. Granddaddy (Max) dropped dead in front of his hardware store caused from "apoplexy" as the heart condition was known. Mother remembers he would go to Houston each year to have blood extracted via leaches. At Grandaddy's death, they were so in debt, Grandmother was left to care for four children and no money. So, Auntie (Cassaline) persuaded her and the children to live with them as she had no children.

"Auntie's husband was a doctor (Dr. Jacob Kelly Gantt). They all lived in a very small house on the bank of the North Edisto River (near Leesville, SC). It was appalling to see, in the thick 'boondock's', a house we would consider a shack by today's standards, three or four rooms in all. But they must have been happy, as mother had very fond memories of life there. The homeplace was known as 'Lower Mills'.

"The next older child, Max, joined the army in WWI. The youngest child, Robert Percy, was in service also in WWI. Grace, the youngest daughter, went to Washington D.C to live with Robert Percy, married and lived there until her death in 1936.

"Grandmother, Rosa Lee, and Max Sternenberg had four children: Viola was born the 17th of October 1890, died the 13th of April 1967 of a heart attack. Grace was born the 17th of December 1895, died the 5th of April 1936 in Washington D.C.

"Grandmother (Rosa Lee) was born the 29th of January 1862. I do not have any info about Grandaddy's side of the family, maybe relatives in Giddings or Paige, Texas."

Signed: Weleska Fulmer Ming (letter written in 1971)

Uncle Leon spoke many times about Aunt Cassaline and the children she helped raise. He said when he was hurt in the 1924 Steedman tornado, he used the same homemade crutches Viola used when she shot her foot. (I bet there's a story there). He also said he went there many times growing up. Cassaline's place was on an island in North Edisto. It was a two-story house, with stairs, part of the stairs was missing in 1930-35. Leon was probably running moonshine stills in that area. Aunt Cassaline died in 1918 and her husband Dr. Gantt died in 1911. It was abandoned and falling down in the early 1930's and was deep in the swamp, away from prying eyes.

My uncle did not quit making moonshine until 1937. Yep, he must have had a still at the Lower Mills. Leon's description of the Lower Mills: "There was an old mill, mill sheet could be seen where the water ran off, to keep from washing a hole in the spillway. Someone had removed partitions out of the old house. The small island where the house stood was in the North Edisto river swamp, surrounded by water when the river was high. The river ran down the east side of the house about 40 yards away. It was on the Lexington side of the river below Convent Church, between Fairview and Wagener, near the Ben Lawson place." I doubt there are any people living now who know where the Ben Lawson place was located.

Aunt Cassaline even taught school during Reconstruction, after the War. She received a Teacher's Second Grade Certificate, dated the 9th of March 1872. She had to pass an examination. Her certificate states, "That Miss Cassaline Gantt having furnished satisfactory evidence of good, moral character, and having passed an examination in Orthography, (I had to look this up, it means a set of conventions for writing a language, including norms of spelling, hyphenation, capitalization, and punctuation). The examination also included reading, writing, arithmetic, geography, and English Grammar." The certificate was only good for one year from date of issue, sounds like she had to be examined again and be recertified. She must have been a really smart lady. I know she loved children because she raised her niece, Rosa Lee, and helped raise Rosa Lee's four children, the Sternenbergs.

7.) Victoria Ann Ceris Gantt was born the 7th of February 1852, died 13th February 1933. Ceris married Eli Abnet "Dikes" Gantt. Aunt Ceris is the daughter of Elijah and Elizabeth Gunter Gantt. Uncle Dikes Gantt was the son of Zimri and Mary Lewis.

My uncle, Leon Gantt, knew Ceris and Dikes personally. He did not remember Elijah and Elizabeth or Zimri and Mary, but he had heard plenty of stories about them. He did tell me Zimri's wife, Mary, was called Aunt Mary Zimri because there was another Mary in the neighborhood at the same time about the same age. Her name was Mary Ann Hall 1842-1936 who married William Henderson Gunter, she was addressed as Aunt Mary Billy to distinguish the two.

Aunt Ceris and Uncle Dikes had eight children. The one I most remember is Max Gantt (1888-1938). Max was a carpenter and he specialized in making chairs, ladder back with a cow hide seat. I know this because I have one of Max's chairs. My Granddaddy, U. Kelly Gantt, purchased some chairs from Max when my Daddy, Robert, was a small boy. My Daddy hammered a bullet casing into the top of one of the back braces of that chair, still there.

Doing the genealogy of the Gantt family in Lexington County is best described as "mass confusion" and I still have the story of the Uly Gantt family of Black Creek to tell.

"Friends come and go; relatives
tend to accumulate."

Elizabeth Bathsheba Gunter Altman, daughter of Elijah Gantt.

Cassaline Gantt, daughter of Elijah, married Dr. Jacob Kelly Gantt.

Lower Mills, home of Cassaline Gantt, daughter of Elijah.

13. The Uly Gantt Family: Life on Black Creek

Ulysses Serenus Gantt married Martha M. Cook, daughter of James and Barbara Posey Cook, in the Fall of 1855. He and Martha had met at a community barn dance in September of that year. It was an unseasonably cold autumn for South Carolina, and the dance was attended by many neighbors and friends in the community. The square dancing seemed to warm the dancers and their cheeks were soon rosy from the motion, or maybe the cold. There were three fires burning brightly in large washtubs on the outer perimeter of the dance area, sand covering the bottom inside. The fires were built on the sand in each tub to prevent the spread of fire to the hay bales the attendees sat upon.

The owner had also assigned a young man to sit close to the tubs to keep the fires burning and for safety sake. That was basically how country folks met the opposite sex in the 19th century, at a barn dance, an Independence Day BBQ, celebration of a wedding, or at a church meeting. There was a full moon that night and Uly asked Martha if she would consider a walk in the fresh air. Martha agreed. As they stood next to the split rail fence beside the barn, brisk breeze blowing, the sharp twang of banjo music seeping through the cracks in the barn walls, she began to pull her shawl closer around her shoulders. "It's a bit chilly," Martha remarked. Uly glanced up, noticing the limbs of the nearby trees swaying in the breeze, and responded, "We best go back inside. It is a bit too cool to be standing out here." That was their beginning.

Uly and Martha married a month later at the home of Elijah and Lizzie. The ceremony was conducted by an itinerary preacher who rode a horse through the district preaching, marrying couples, and presiding over funerals. Martha's parents, James and Barbara, attended. Her sister, Amanda, and her husband, Cary Rawls, were also in attendance. Uly and his new brother-in-law, Cary, would become fast friends and cohorts.

On the 7th of September 1856, Martha gave birth to their first child, Jacob Kelly Gantt, called Kell from birth. Martha and Uly lived in a small two story clapboard house on the bank of what was called Little Black Creek, a tributary of the bigger waterway known as Big Black Creek. This tributary then merged and flowed into the North Edisto River.

The house where Kell was born was constructed by Uly, with help from his brother-in-law, Cary Rawls, and brothers, Elijah M., Adolphus, Caswell, and Ravonell, wonderful carpenters all. There was a winding staircase that led to a floor above, containing two sleeping chambers, intended for their children. The main level included Uly and Martha's bed chamber, a hall with outside doors on either end of the hall and a separate dining room. If there was a breeze from the flowing creek, the door towards the creek allowed a wind tunnel effect through the hall and helped cool the dining area. Toward the back, a door led across a covered walkway to a separate kitchen house thirty feet away. The dining area in the main house was large, the ceiling high to allow better cooling in the muggy South Carolina summers. The outside doors, back and front, allowed any breath of cool air to pass through.

Uly even built a fan, rigged a line to the wall where a lever could be pumped up and down sweeping his fan invention back and forth above the table. This stirred the air and cooled overheated folks eating hot foods. All that was needed was a volunteer to operate the fan during meals. The older children would take turns working the fan. They probably didn't have a choice in the volunteering part.

The kitchen house out back had a wood burning cook stove, fireplace, cook table, and pantry with shelves for staples... flour, cane sugar, salt, and such. The pantry also contained a salt box to preserve meat and shelving to place jars of canned vegetables from their substantial vegetable garden. The ceiling of the kitchen house was open above, only the large ceiling beams exposed. The separate kitchen house added safety from fire and the open ceiling helped the cooks survive the steamy temperatures in the unforgiveable summer heat.

Three other sons were born to Uly and Martha before "the War" would take Uly away from his family. Those three sons were: Luther Lafayette born the 7th of March 1858,

Jefferson Davis born the 13th of October 1859, and Oliver Cromwell born the 31st of August 1861. Uly joined the Confederate Army on the 3rd of January 1862. His service was discussed in Chapter 11 when I covered 'The War'.

On the 26th day of October 1860, Ulysses S. Gantt and his cohort and brother-in-law, Cary Rawls, took it upon themselves to mortgage 2,200 acres of land on little Black Creek to James D. Jones for two thousand seven hundred and fifty dollars. This land was the entitled inheritance of their wives Martha and Amanda from their Cook Family. Evidently, their wives were not aware of this transaction. Later this deception would cause Martha and Uly problems. Elijah Gantt, Uly's father, even signed as witness to the mortgage.

At that period in time, women had few legal rights. I'm certain Elijah thought nothing of the mortgage, probably didn't think that mortgaging the Cook family land was a problem for his son, Uly, and friend, Cary. The two young men had big goals to accomplish for themselves and their families with the money. They were hoping to build a pond and grist mill in the run of Black Creek or maybe a sawmill, maybe both. They wanted to be self-sufficient and build something that they and their families would be proud of. Then in December 1860, South Carolina seceded from the Union. In quick succession, like dominos, the other Southern states followed. Paying "one half of the mortgage amount, namely one thousand three hundred and seventy-five dollars in twelve months plus interest" was going to be an impossible task.

Martha and the boys Kell, Luther, Davis, and Crummy fared pretty well during the War. The boys, the older three, did the farming along with their mother. The house was so far off any main wagon roads and trails living down on Little Black Creek, the Yankees didn't harass them or destroy their homes and fields. They lived at the 'back side of nowhere'. When they had to go to a general store for supplies, which was not very often, that was the only time they heard any news about the War.

Sometimes Elijah and Lizzie visited and brought Martha and the boys some butchered meat, smoked or salted. Towards the end of the War, Kell and Luther caught rabbits in snares and boxes they set in the woods. Their grandfather, Elijah, taught them how to shoot, kill, prepare, and preserve their game, most caught and shot in the woods across the creek. They were not rich, but always had plenty of food and the boys were old enough to cut and split wood for the fireplaces and the wood cook stove. Wood produced their heat in the winter and fuel for the cookstove. Cutting trees and splitting wood was a year-round job. Uly was off fighting the War and the boys had to do what their father would if he were there.

Martha's mother, Barbara Cook, visited once on a Sunday and spent the night with her daughter, but James, her father, had passed away in 1858. Barbara couldn't visit any more, she was almost sixty years old, and her health was beginning to decline. Martha's sister, Louamma Jane, still lived at home with Momma Cook, but the three Cook brothers were away fighting in the War.

Uly returned home after the surrender of the Confederate Army and was welcomed by his wife, Martha, and their four boys. After his return, their family grew by three more children.

The Children of Ulysses S. Gantt were:

1. Jacob Kelly Gantt was born on the 7th of September 1856. Kell as he was called was my great grandfather. Kell Gantt and family were covered in my first book, _Where Memories Live_ and the second, _The Return Home_. He died of a stroke in 1930 and is buried at Pine Grove Baptist Church, near Fairview.
2. Luther Lafayette Gantt was born the 7th of March 1858.
3. Jefferson Davis Gantt was born the 13th of October 1859.
4. Oliver Cromwell Gantt was born 31st August 1861 "Crummy".
5. Ella Jane Gantt was born 2nd March 1866.
6. Corrie Gantt was born 1867.
7. Elijah Serenus Gantt "Babe" was born 23rd of February 1869. He was always called Babe for an obvious reason; he was the baby of Uly and Martha's family.

"Children must be taught how to
think, not what to think."

—Margaret Mead

Martha Matilda Cook Gantt, wife of Uly Gantt.

14. Lumber Rafting on the Edisto River

I will begin by telling you what little I remember from my childhood of waters and streams. Across the field and down the slope behind that old house I grew up in was a stream and swampy area called Coon branch. We, as children, went there often and traced it to its source or the head as it was called. I remember finding the spring that fed the standing water. The water was not a pond, it was wide, but not very deep. We called it a branch. The spring where water bubbled up from the ground in boiling white sand was the beginning of the branch.

It was even dammed up at one time to create a pond. I don't remember when, before my time, but I do remember walking on the remnants of the dam. I was told it blew out one Sunday morning. It was an earthen dam, about four feet high in my youth, and a stream still ran between the two mounds that remained. This dam was never rebuilt. The stream surrounded the juniper trees in a swampy area further down. In rainy weather, the trees were standing in water. As kids, we just thought it was a fun place to play.

The sand hills of South Carolina hold many springs. They are the beginning of ponds if a dam is built and the area below cleared. Eventually these small streams fill the pond area. A spillway is needed to control the water level and the runoff, especially in rainy weather. The runoff dumps excess water which eventually flows into rivers. Ponds are where grist mills and sawmills were once located.

In my childhood, I remember the remains of many sawmills. There were always the spongelike remains of sawdust piles that we walked over, sinking in at each step. In my youth and even today, lumber is easily transported on big log trucks, or trains. Sawmills can be anywhere; transportation is not a problem.

When I was probably six, my Uncle Leon sold his timber for two thousand dollars cash. He showed us kids the money. We had never heard of anyone having that much cash.

I remember a makeshift pen made by nailing slabs to a group of trees. Two mules were kept in that pen at the end of a day's work. The mules were used to drag the large limbed up pine logs out of the swamp to the sawmill, about 200 yards to the north.

What I remember most is the whining sound of the saw as the logs were pushed through. The outside of the pines was discarded as slabs, mostly used for warming the house in winter. My uncle, I recall, named at least three branches: Coon branch, Pitt branch and Rattlesnake branch. These were spring fed swampy areas where water stood, year-round.

The tank place was so called because the water tower for the train once stood there. This same spring, at the tank place, was called Zeke's landing. There may have been a creek there and a place to put boats in, as the name implies. A stream that flowed from this spring flowed through a pipe near Steedman and fed into Hall's pond. Hall's pond was big enough to even have a small island, about one hundred acres. There are many springs in the sandhills of mid-South Carolina, therefore, it was not a big problem to build dams and create ponds.

A big pond was created on Black Creek to support Uly and Cary's timber business. A dam was built across the creek, two springs fed water into the area above the dam. Large trees had to be cut down and the area dug out manually to scoop a bowl shape area for the springs to fill. Building the pond required a large force of workers. They had to be paid, but after the War ended, men were willing to work hard jobs sunup to sundown to put food on the table for their families.

The trees were cut but the stumps were left and would be underwater. Both springs produced a natural water source, and a rapid stream began to run through the pond area. It did not take long to have a viable pond with a spill-way that could lower the level in the pond while releasing a large volume of water down the creek.

Uly Gantt, Cary Rawls, Uly's sons, Kell, Davis, Luther, and Crummy and his uncles, helped with the sawmill and building the rafts. Elijah Monroe, Uly's brother, was well versed in the mechanics of sawmilling and helped set up a sawmill on the banks of the pond.

In the late 19th century, before railroads became an important mode of transporting lumber to market, the Edisto river flowing from the sandhills to the coast was the best way to transport lumber. The Gantts sawmill and lumber operation was located on Big Black Creek. Before the journey to the coast began, Uly would send two boats with two workers in each, along with saws and axes. Their job was to make sure there were no fallen trees, large limbs, or any other objects that might hinder the rafts. They had to go down Big Black Creek to the confluence of the North Edisto. Then make sure the North Edisto was clear of debris until the point, near Branchville, where the North and South Edisto joined to form the Edisto River. When they reached the Edisto, it being much wider, they could return home. They walked home from Branchville. That was at least 140 years ago.

The nearest market for selling their lumber was Charleston. Therefore, lumber rafts were made, and lumber transported down rivers on the rafts to the coast. It was the fastest and easiest way to go. In that time period, the sawmill needed to be located near the pond where the raft was assembled, so that the lumber did not have to be transported far to be put on the raft, it could be handed down by workers.

The construction of the rafts was complicated. They were assembled below the dam and the spillway, on a sloping bank of Big Black Creek. The bottom was split pine logs, the round half on the bottom for buoyancy, then a layer of thick, rough lumber. There were stanchions, hammered through the rough lumber and into the pine logs on the bottom, they were located on the outside, front, back, and center, six stanchions for each raft. It had to be a tight fit, sometimes wedges were pounded at the base of these sturdy wooden poles to be sure the stanchions were snug and immovable.

The rafts were normally six feet wide, but the length could be longer depending on the lumber being loaded. The lumber was rafted down river in February and March, no mosquitoes, and it gave workers something to do to earn their pay in the off season.

Before the journey began, three boards were removed from the spillway, allowing water from the pond to rush into Black Creek. The rising water level made it easier to launch the rafts and move them down the creek. When there was no breeze to push the raft downstream, men on the raft used long poles to push the raft manually. These poles would be placed in the creek, on either side of the raft until the workers felt contact with the bottom. They then pushed with all their might to move the raft forward.

When the raft was moving under wind power, they could warm beside the large wash tub placed in the center of each raft. Sand covered the bottom of each tub, and a fire was built. Cold was a big problem and the men dressed accordingly, thick britches and long-sleeved flannel shirts, topped with a heavy denim coat lined in wool.

Late in the evenings, they would maneuver the raft to the riverbank and tie it to a large tree. This kept the raft from floating down stream. Here on the riverbank, they would build a fire, make their coffee, and eat their supper, usually cold cornpone, and smoked meat. Food for their trip was packed in knap sacks like those used during the War, simple food that would not spoil. Broken branches from the ground were gathered and stacked on the raft. This would be their fuel for the fire built in the wash tubs the next morning.

It was approximately a one-hundred-and-twenty-mile journey to Edisto Island. The trip, depending on the wind and weather, could be four to six weeks. When they finally got there, an area that the city had set aside on the edge of the river surrounded by pilings and called 'the Bull Pen' was their destination. All rafts were poled into this area and tied off. The owner of the rafts or their representatives, Uly, and sons Kell and Luther would go directly to the Broker's Office. All interested parties came to evaluate the lumber and offer a price.

After business was settled, the men walked home or took the train to Aiken. I don't know which. Walking was cheaper, but they were all bone tired, cold from the wind off the beaches, and just wanted to be back home. Since they now had money, Uly, may have paid for the train to Aiken.

"There are no shortcuts to any place worth going."

—Beverly Sills

15. Jacob Kelly Gantt, son of Uly and Martha

The children of Uly and Martha grew up in Lexington County. The oldest, Jacob Kelly, "Kell", was my great grandfather. His wife, Peninnah Woodward Gantt was the daughter of Thomas Jefferson Woodward and Ara Gunter. Earlier I spoke of Peninnah as a child in the original home at Rayflin, living there during the 'War' with her grandparents, Russell, and Elizabeth Nelson Gunter. Grandmama Peninnah lived her whole life in that old house at Rayflin beside the North Edisto River, from May of 1860 through the middle of November 1949.

People in modern America, I'm sure, will find it hard to believe someone living all those years in the same old house in the back woods far from civilization was happy with her life. I believe Peninnah was, from the stories I have been told.

The original two room house had been expanded in the 1890's. The original two-room version was swallowed up by added rooms but was still there. My Daddy, Robert Kelly

Gantt, said he could remember as a child there was a spiral staircase leading to a sleeping loft in those beginning two rooms. The original was built when Russell and Elizabeth lived there and had a rock chimney near the road.

I visited there many times as a child. There is no way to pinpoint when the original house was built, but if it was built before Russell and Elizabeth were married, it was built before 1806, the birth of their oldest child. In the early 1980's the house burned, only the rock chimney stood and the bedroom to the left of the front room, an added addition from the 1890's.

Kell was a big farmer. Uncle Leon said he owned a five-mule farm. I still am not sure exactly what that meant. I believe it just referred to a big farming operation at that time and at least five mules were plowed in the Spring to do the necessary planting. Kell had a lot of farm equipment, plows, hay rakes, wagons, mule harness, saddles, and sleds for moving equipment more easily. There was a corncrib across the road, a big barn, fenced pastures, and fields for planting. Granddaddy Kell also owned a set of blacksmithing tools.

Most of my stories have been passed down through Kell and Peninnah's grandsons, my Uncle Leon, and my Daddy, Robert. They both had fantastic memories and Uncle Leon loved to tell stories. Leon Gantt was a phenomenal storyteller, and I was his constant companion as a child. I talk about my Gantt family in my earlier books, *Where Memories Live* and *The Return Home*. I started writing about their lives through these stories my Uncle and Daddy told my siblings and me.

After Uncle Leon passed away in 2002, I decided to write about their lives to preserve what I had learned. I never knew Kell or Peninnah, I didn't even know my grandfather, Ulysess Kelly Gantt, called Kelly. Granddaddy Kelly died in December 1950; I was born in October of the following year. I do, however, feel I did know him, because of all the stories I have heard about the moonshine stills he ran along with his brothers in the swamps of the North Edisto River. I do remember my Granddaddy Kelly's brothers, my Uncles, Sammy and Rion and my Aunt Corrie Gantt Smith and of course, Aunt Jennie Gantt Rish. Aunt Jennie lived until 1985.

My uncle's stories were fascinating and I, always a lover of history, collected their stories on audio tape or wrote them down. I was bitten by the genealogy bug in 1970 and did all my research before the internet existed. I did lots of research in archives, courthouses, and cemeteries, I also interviewed every old person that was related to my family and took notes of those interviews in spiral notebooks. I guess I earned the title of Family Historian.

I also made scrapbooks, containing many old family pictures. Then, in 2017, I began in earnest to organize and tell these stories in book form. I have published four, this prequel will be the fifth.

Children of Jacob Kelly "Kell" Gantt and Peninnah Woodward Gantt:

1. Thomas Roston Gantt born 1878, died 1951.
2. Jacob Cyrus Gantt born 1881, died 1965.

3. Ulysses Kelly Gantt born 1883, died 1950. My grandfather.
4. Corrie Ella Gantt born 1886, died 1964.
5. Samuel Layfette born 1889, died 1965.
6. Andrew Woodward "Woodard" Gantt born 1892, died 1939.
7. Virginia Hersey Gantt born 1895, died 1985.
8. Rion Tillman Gantt born 1898, died 1966.
9. Delphin Delmas Gantt "Buck" born 1900, died 1935.

"Rejoice with your family in the
beautiful land of life."

—Albert Einstein

Jacob Kelly 'Kell' Gantt, great grandfather of the author.

Peninnah Woodward Gantt, wife of Kell Gantt,
great grandmother of the author.

Original home of Kell and Peninnah Gantt, at Rayflin

Kell and Peninnah Woodward Gantt, child is Woodard ca. 1892.

Ulysses Kelly Gantt, son of Kell Gantt, grandfather of the author.

16. Luther Layfette Gantt, son of Uly and Martha

Luther Layfette Gantt, from the very start, helped his father, Uly, run the sawmill on Black Creek and rafted lumber to Charleston. Luther married Alice A. Rawls, daughter of Arthur Henry Rawls. Her father was killed in the War at Petersburg, Virginia on the 10th of June 1865.

Luther and Alice married about 1880, their home was in the Black Creek area. He followed his father, Uly, in the timber and farming business. In cold weather, Luther and his workers rafted his lumber to Charleston, selling it there, just like his father, and took the train back, getting off at Montmorenci where I now live. I believe during that time period, late 19th century, it was called Johnson's Turnout. Luther then walked from here back to his farm on Black Creek, about thirty miles. It's hard for modern day Americans to believe, people walked that far to get home.

I remember my Uncle Leon walked everywhere he went unless my Daddy Robert was available to drive him. Leon never had a driver's license. But he never walked anything compared to thirty miles, every place he wanted to go was within five miles of home.

Aubrey Gantt, a dear friend, and distant cousin, stated that he and his parents visited his Grandfather and Grandmother, Luther, and Alice, frequently at their farm on Black Creek. His grandmother, Alice, was a wonderful storyteller. Sometimes Luther's brothers would be visiting also, especially Uncle Davis, Uncle Crummy, and Uncle Babe. Crummy and Babe lived closer, near Black Creek and Uncle Davis never stayed in one place for very long. Brother Kell was busy with the farm, spring planting time, summer tending the fields and picking vegetables. Late fall and early winter were butchering time. Kell and Peninnah were too busy surviving to visit family for socializing. They went to church on Sundays. That was the day they rested from their labors.

Aubrey asked Grandmother Alice if Yankee soldiers came to their home when Sherman marched to the sea. She replied, "They did, but there was nothing for them to take. We had advanced warning and two of the family's slaves took our livestock and hid them in the swamp. Any other valuables were buried. Even the hams and smoked and salted meats were hidden in a small underground cellar. One Yankee even picked me up and said, 'This is a small Rebel.' They milled around in the house and yard, then rode away. The Rawls, Alice's family, lived on the North Edisto River

Alice, Luther's wife, told Aubrey about the time the whole family attended the Centennial celebration in Aiken, the one hundredth birthday of America. Alice said she was just a young girl, and the speaker was the Governor and former general in the Confederate Army, General Wade Hampton III. General Hampton served as SC governor from 1876 until 1879. Alice also remembered what was considered an important message to renegades and those that broke the law, a public hanging. It was the finale of the program. They may have had a fireworks display, probably not just firecrackers or roman candles, more likely gun powder and dynamite.

It seems that Luther and the outlaw, Emmanuel Williams, were not only first cousins, but also good friends. Late one evening, Emmanuel knocked on Luther's door. He needed a place to lay low out of the public eye for a few days, he had a flesh wound from some run in with the law. He, of course, was a wanted man and the law was looking for him. Alice told Luther that Emmanuel could not be around their children, but he could stay in the barn, and they would send him food.

So, Emmanuel was furnished blankets to make his bed in the hay loft and food was sent out to him. He stayed about a week and then disappeared. Emmanuel was a great marksman. He could ride a horse around a tree as fast as he could go and with his pistol, shoot all the bark off a large pine tree at eye level. Emmanuel did confess to Luther that he had stolen Crummy's rifle, saying he didn't have any great use for it. Emmauel was later killed in Seivern, SC in 1895. I have heard it said, "Those who live by the gun, die by the gun."

Luther Lafayette Gantt, born the 7th of March 1858, died the 9th of March 1932, married Alice A. Rawls, born the 27th of December 1862, died the 10th of June 1946. Their children were:

1.) George Carl Gantt, born the 18th of October 1882, died the 15th of November 1939.

2.) Clara Gantt, born the 29th of October 1886, died the 11th of November 1953, married Adam Clifton Smith.

3.) Roxie Gantt, born the 17th of February 1889, died the 3rd of January 1981, married late in life to William O'Neal Smith, they had no children. Aubrey said his Aunt Roxie was a wonderful lady who always treated family as guests. At thirteen, Aubrey went to visit Aunt Roxie for a couple of days. Uncle Neal, her husband, was a proficient marksman. He took Aubrey to a nearby field to teach him how to handle and shoot the shotgun. Aunt Roxie gave Aubrey some parting advice. "Be careful and don't shoot yourself. If you have to, shoot Neal instead."

4.) Grover Gantt, born the 20th of October 1892, died the 21st of June 1954, Grover married Blanche Holley. Grover and Blanche were the parents of Aubrey Gantt who I spoke of earlier. Grover was a veteran of WWI; Blanche was a substitute teacher at Pelion Elementary. I remember she substituted for Miss Maude Shumpert while she was out sick when I was in the 3rd grade. I was very excited to meet Miss Blanche. She was, after all, kin. Aubrey was a super great guy. I met him in the early 1980's, he and his wife Jane came to one of our Gantt reunions. He was a medical doctor in Williston, S.C. He was a very dedicated doctor and all his patients in Williston appreciated his candor and bedside manner. When he retired, I attended his retirement party at the Town Hall building in Williston. I met his three children there, Doyle, George, and Becky. The first Christmas card I received every year was simply signed Aubrey and Jane. He would stop by often and tell me family stories. He told me once he was out by the road planting flowers, in tattered work clothes, sweaty and dirty. A lady pulled up in a fancy car and beckoned him with a wave. How much do you charge to do yard work? She asked with a look of disdain on her face. Aubrey replied, "The lady who lives here lets me sleep with her." With a "Well, I never!" she sped away in her fancy car. Truc or not, he was a quick thinker and had a comeback for a snobbish woman.

5.) Jennings Bryan Gantt, born the 12th of April 1896, died the 10th of February 1941, married Evelyn Susie Hall.

6.) Ida Gantt, born the 21st of January 1899, died the 7th of January 1979. she first married J.H. Buice and second Shellie Fulmer. She had no children.

7.) Theodore Roosevelt Gantt, born the 30th of June 1901, died the 5th of January 1950; he married Ava Lee Yonce.

8.) Sue Gantt, born the 4th of February 1905, died 1st of August 1991. Sue married Jewell M. Boone Sr. I spoke with Sue Boone on the phone before her death, don't remember what she told me about her family but I'm sure there are notes somewhere from my conversation with Miss Sue, probably in one of my many spiral notebooks.

Most of the eight children of Luther and Alice attended either Pelion or Fairview Schools. I attended Pelion and wrote an article for the spiral bound book published by The Pelion History Committee in 1984 about the Gantt Family. Looking at the published book recently, I realized I was related to most of the students at Pelion school. Cousins of some sort, still kin.

> "My kinfolks thought more about character
> than culture. They said culture could be
> acquired, but character had to be formed.
> Character had to be hammered into shape
> like hot iron on an anvil. It had to be molded
> in the most exact and unrelenting form."
>
> —Ben Robertson

Luther Lafayette Gantt, son of Uly and Martha Gantt.

Alice Rawls Gantt, wife of Luther.

Aubrey Gantt and wife Jane, grandson of Luther and Alice Gantt.

17. Jefferson Davis Gantt, Growing up on Black Creek

Davis Gantt was born in October of 1859 at the homestead on Little Black Creek, only two years before The War. Their father, Uly, joined the Confederate Army in January 1862 and life changed for Martha and her boys. She was left with four young children, Kell being the oldest, age six. Luther was four and the two youngest, Davis barely two, and Crummy, a five-month-old baby, could not remember their father, Uly, until the War was over. Their mother, Martha, babied the two youngest in the absence of their father. Davis had a great childhood with his brothers Kell, Luther, and Crummy. They could only remember playing in the creek, skipping stones across the dark water, and as they grew older, wading in the water, practicing floating on their backs, and being taught how to swim by their older brothers.

There was a large oak standing on the creek bank, a big limb hanging out over the water. Their two older brothers decided, when the weather was hot, they would rig up a rope swing. Kell shimmied up the big oak, toe hold after toe hold until he reached the limb, carrying the end of a thick rope between his teeth. The excess he curled like a necklace over his head and around his neck.

Reaching the big limb, he tied the rope around the limb securely, dropping the rest to the bank below. Luther grabbed the rope as Kell dropped it and tied a big loop at the end. The rope swing would always be one of the memories all the boys carried from childhood on the creek. They would put one foot in the rope loop, grab further up on the rope and with their other foot push out over the water, turn loose in the middle of the creek, dropping with a big splash into the cold water. That was the summer of 1863.

When the War ended in 1865, all the boys helped their father in the timber business and farming. Three other children were born to Uly and Martha after the War, Ella Jane, Corrie, and Elijah Serenus 'Babe'. As the children grew, they married and started their own families, always living in the Black Creek area. Jefferson Davis 'Davis' Gantt, being the exception. He was somewhat of a vagabond, married three times, visited his siblings, lived for a time in Florida and in Alabama. They never knew when Davis would show up or where he had been. I have a photo of Uncle Davis sitting on the back porch, feet on the top step beside my great grandfather, Kell Gantt. Davis has a hat on and is sporting a handlebar mustache.

Jefferson Davis Gantt was born on the 13th of October 1859 and died the 27th of November 1937. He married first Marietta Rawls and had one daughter with Marietta.

1.) Desiree "Dessie" Olive Gantt, born the 30th of November 1885 in Lexington County, SC, died 9th of January 1923, married John Swinton Jeffcoat and had eleven children. Dessie died and is interred in the Able Cemetery, Gantt, Alabama.

Davis second wife was Allie Sternenberg, and his third wife was Nan Garrick. Davis is buried beside his third wife, Nannie Garrick Gantt in Elmwood Cemetery, Columbia, SC.

> "The Memories we make with
> our family is everything."
>
> —Candace Cameron Bure

Jefferson Davis Gantt, son Uly Gantt.

18. Oliver Cromwell Gantt, A Baby When Father Went to War

Oliver Cromwell Gantt, "Crummy" as he was referred to was considered to be a small man, barely over five feet when an adult. When his father left for the War, he was a five-month-old infant. Uncle Crummy was born the 31st of August 1861 at the homeplace of his father, Ulysses "Uly" and mother, Martha Cook.

After the War, he helped his father, Uly, farm and in the timber business. Crummy would marry Anna Priscilla Lucas about 1885, apparently a small person also. In one interview I conducted with my step grandfather, Frank Gantt, he spoke of Crummy and Cilla as small, almost like little dolls. Priscilla was born the 7th of July 1867 and died the 2nd of December 1909. She died at age 42 and Uncle Crummy lived to the age of 92, fifty years after his wife died. I have heard my Uncle speak often of Uncle Crummy. I can remember seeing his son, Monroe, at Pine Grove Baptist Church and the part about Crummy and Cilla being small people, their son, Monroe was shorter than I am.

He lived to be 98 years old. Monroe married Ethel Boat-wright. They had no children.

I do have one story my Uncle Leon shared about Babe and Crummy, I believe it bears repeating. I heard this story from my uncle more than once and he would laugh every time he told it.

"The whole family was busy working in the fields. Crummy was left to tend to Babe in the kitchen house while their mother was in the vegetable garden. This would have been about 1872 when Babe was barely three, too little to be left by himself safely. Crummy was ten and was the designated babysitter.

"There was an empty wooden box, the kind fruit was shipped in at that time. Crummy spied it under the cook table. It was a sturdy box; Crummy pulled it out from under the small table. Babe immediately wanted to get in the box and have Crummy push him around on the wooden plank floor. It wasn't hard to slide the box. Ma had swept the floor good, just before she went outside.

"Babe hopped into the box and Crummy began to push him all over the kitchen house. Babe laughing, thought it was great fun. After pushing the box with Babe sitting inside, Crummy got tired. Crummy was a small boy, even though he was older than Babe.

"'Get out of the box Babe,' Crummy demanded, 'you can push me.' Even at age three, 'he was a stubborn little shit', as Crummy described the baby of the family. He knew his Ma, Martha, would wash his mouth out with soap if she heard his description of little brother. Well, Babe, flat refused to budge from the box.

"Over in a corner of the far wall, Crummy spied a short wooden barrel. He knew immediately it contained gun powder. Smiling to himself, he thought, *I'll fix you, Babe*! He went over to the box, pried the top off, reached in, and got a handful. Babe had gotten out of the box, curious as to what Crummy was about. Crummy lifted the box and poured the gunpowder in a little mound with a line running about three inches across the floor.

"'Get in the box, Babe.' Babe got in the box expecting to be pushed some more. A box of long kitchen matches was on a ledge near the cook table and Crummy retrieved two, just in case the first didn't spark. With Babe in the wooden box gripping the sides, ready for a ride, Crummy lit the gunpowder. With the spark, the box leaped about three feet in the air. Babe erupted in laughter; it was so much fun. Babe still refused to get out of the box and give Crummy a turn. 'Do it again, Crummy, do it again!' *We'll see about that* Crummy thought. With the other match still in his dungaree pocket, he said, 'Move the box, Babe. I'll give you another ride.' He walked back to the barrel, and this time, Crummy got a double handful of gun powder.

"He carefully placed a bigger pile on the floor, 'Get back in the box, Babe.' When Crummy lit the gunpowder this time, the wooden box jumped more than six feet, thankfully between the exposed beams above. On the way down, Babe's pants caught on a pot hook, and he was suspended above the floor, bawling his eyes out. Martha heard all the commotion coming from the kitchen house and ran to investigate. She found Babe hanging on the pot hook, the smell of gunpowder permeating the air, the box slung against the wall and a couple of chairs turned over. Crummy was nowhere in sight. Babe seemed to be in one piece, tears dripping off his chin and him blubbering about how badly Crummy had scared him.

"Heading out the back door, Martha spied Crummy up in a big oak tree. She shouted, 'Young man get down from that tree, right now. You could have killed your little brother. You are going to get the whipping you deserve.' Crummy didn't budge from his perch, so Martha turned and headed for the cane patch.

"With the pocketknife that she always carried in her apron pocket; she sawed a long thin cane pole. Going back to the tree, she repeated her demand to Crummy. No response, so she decided to try jugging him from the tree with the pole. (this meaning in the South, she attempted to punch him with the cane). Crummy maneuvered about on the lower limbs until he thought he was low enough to jump, pretend he had broken his arm, and convince Ma he was really hurt, winning her sympathy for her injured son.

"When he jumped, he screamed and grabbed his arm shouting, 'My arm must be broke, Ma!' Crummy was a good actor and stunt man and Ma swallowed his pleas, hook line and sinker. 'I'll send, your brother Kell for Dr. Gantt, he lives not two miles from here!'

"When Dr. Gantt arrived thirty minutes later, Crummy was laying on a mat in the kitchen house, his Ma hovering over him, tears in her eyes. Dr. Gantt told Martha to go outside, and he would examine Crummy. 'Don't worry Martha, I'm sure the boy will be fine.' As soon as Ma had departed, 'Crummy explained to Dr. Gantt, who was married to Aunt Cassaline, his Pa Uly's sister, the whole sad story and how he didn't mean to hurt Babe, only wanted to teach him a lesson, 'I'm not really hurt, doctor, just trying to avoid a whipping from Ma.' Dr. Gantt put Crummy's arm in a sling, told Martha he would be fine, just needed a few days rest and gave her some white pills to relieve Crummy's pain."

My uncle, Leon Gantt, loved to repeat this story. I believe it is probably mostly true, stories always seem to be embellished to make them more interesting. If the gunpowder part is true, it needed no more embellishments. I do know about children doing crazy things to entertain themselves and others. In my childhood, we had to have an imagination and not look at any activity as dangerous, having a picnic in the swamp in the middle of a muggy summer or riding a bicycle, no helmet and no hands on the handlebars flying down a hill. Danger was far from our minds! It was all about the thrill and the fun! I believe Uncle Babe had too big a thrill from his ride up through the rafters.

Children of Oliver Cromwell and Annie Priscilla Lucas:

1. Monroe Gantt, born the 7th of November 1886, died the 25th of January 1985.
2. Ulysses Hudson Gantt, born 2nd of November 1888, died 30th June 1989.
3. Willie Clemson Gantt, born 24th of June 1894, died 27th February 1979.

4. Ethel Mae Gantt, born the 15th of September 1896, died 19th of July 1999.
5. Carrie Etheridge Gantt, born the 25th of January 1899, died 6th March 1989.
6. Davis Houston Gantt, born 1st of June 1901, died 10th November 1910.
7. John Walter Gantt, born 6th of November 1902, died the 11th of May 1941.
8. Ruby Elizabeth Gantt, born the 19th of March 1904, died 19th March 1987.
9. Wyman Gantt, born 9th of April 1906, died 1951.
10. Their mother, Annie Pricilla Lucas Gantt, died in December 1909. The youngest child was three years old, there were two other children under ten years old. Uncle Crummy must have had a hard time raising all his children.

"Short People: God only lets things
grow until they are perfect … Some of
us didn't take as long as others!"

Martha Matilda Cook Gantt, wife of Uly.

Family of Oliver Cromwell 'Crummy' Gantt with his children, each of his children is marked with an asterisk.

Family of Crummy Gantt, son of Uly and Martha. His wife, Priscilla in the back holding their baby.

19. Daughters of Uly and Martha, Rural Life During the War

When Uly went to War in 1862, Martha was left to fend for herself and her boys. She had four children at home, all boys under age ten. She and her boys had a lot to do to survive and to feed themselves. Kell, the oldest, was only six, Luther was four, but both boys helped her with whatever she asked of them. They were young, but they helped her carry baskets of vegetables from the garden and buckets of water from the creek up to the house. They could dump the water buckets in the two big wash tubs on the wide bench, in the back yard. Once a week was wash day and she did the wash with a scrub board and a bar of homemade soap, given to her by her mother or her mother-in-law, Lizzie. Lizzie and Elijah's children were out on their own or in the War, like Uly. She did not trust the boys to actually wash the clothes, but they did most of the water carrying, most importantly they could keep an eye on Davis and Crummy when she had chores outside.

Once a week, Martha insisted the boys had to have a bath in the kitchen house. The water for their bath was dipped from the rain barrels at the corner of the kitchen, when it stormed, and rain poured, the rain barrels would be filled by the runoff from the roof. They would always complain, "Ma why, do we have to have a bath every week? Other children in the country don't bathe every week."

Martha always replied, "y'all are not other children, you are my children, you will take a bath once a week. In the summer, you can bathe in the creek, but the rest of the year you will bathe in the kitchen house, I will heat a pot of water on the wood stove to make the bath more comfortable."

So, year-round, once a week, the children would take a bath. They took turns and used the same water, maybe with a little more heated water added. That is where the saying, "don't throw the baby out with the bath water" comes from. Everybody used the same bath water, oldest to youngest.

The boys loved their mother and even at a young age they knew, she was to be obeyed. Finally, Uly got home from the War and the boys were older and could help their father in the fields.

* * * * *

In March 1866, Martha and Uly had a daughter, Ella Jane, and from the beginning she was a precious little girl. Martha was so glad to have another girl in the house and as soon as Ella could toddle around, she was always following in her mother's footsteps, usually holding on to her apron strings. As she grew, Ella and her mother grew closer. Ella wanted to help her mother. By age two, she was Martha's little helper, she tried to be anyway. She would wrap her short arms around her mother's leg and throw kisses when Martha sat her on a stool beside the table. Ella was just beginning to put words together. She was a smart child, but her older brothers pretty much ignored her as a whiny little brat. Crummy, at age four, played a lot with little Ella, especially a game of chase and he would try to pick her up and carry her. Ella found him very funny and would laugh when Crummy played pick a boo and hid from her. He was not hard to find, but he loved that he could make Ella laugh. Her other brothers had too many chores with their father to play with their little sister, except for Crummy.

Pretty soon, Martha was expecting again. Only a year after Ella, Corrie was born. Martha was extremely pleased to have another little girl to follow in her footsteps and to one day be a help with the chores all women had to contend with. Martha was, of course, responsible for the cooking, washing clothes and dishes, mending and cleaning house. That was the lot of all wives and mothers in the late 19th century, there were few modern inventions then. She realized her husband had his hands full with the timber business, blacksmithing, carpentry, and farming. She and the younger children, Crummy, Davis and the girls, were responsible for the vegetable garden. Davis and Crummy milked their two old cows, Bessie and Sukey, and fed the chickens that ranged free in the yard. When the girls started helping, they were taught to cook and would take their small wicker baskets to the little house where the chickens lived. They made their nests in the cubby holes that covered the back wall top to bottom, each was filled with straw. There they would gather the eggs and put them in their baskets. When the sunset in the evenings, the chickens were called to their house and the door was firmly shut, a cast iron fire poker propped against the door latch. Martha didn't want any foxes to get in the henhouse and kill the chickens.

They depended on their livestock, cows, and chickens for food, mules and horses for transportation and plowing the fields. In the Spring, Uly, Kell and Luther laid out, plowed, and planted the vegetable garden for Martha. The younger children were then in charge of picking, washing, and preparing the vegetables as they came in. Martha directed the cooking and her and the girls, shelled peas, beans and decided what to cook and how. Martha appreciated the fresh vegetables and never complained but it seemed to her that every plant produced at the same time. Every day, especially after a rain shower, the vegetables had to be picked and prepared. There was also the canning, preparing for Winter when there would be no vegetables from their garden.

The crops planted by Uly in the fields, he and the older boys managed and harvested. They planted wheat, corn, and cotton. Wheat was cut with long-bladed scythes, they then bounded the sheaves together by hand and spread a white sheet on the barn floor. The sheaves were pounded on the sheet separating the seed-heads from the seed covering and the stalks. The stalks were used as bedding for their animals in the barn stalls. The seeds were separated from the husks by using a winnowing tray on a windy day, the farmers would toss the mixed chaff and grains repeatedly into the air. The wind would blow the chaff away, as the good kernels of grain fell into the tray. The good kernels were poured into large baskets to be sold to the flour mill located in Lexington. Often the farmers received a portion of the ground flour as part of their pay. Families used so much flour at that time, biscuits or flapjacks were a necessity of every meal, the flour was dumped in a barrel underneath the cook table in the kitchen house. Sacks of flour were stored in the root cellar, keeping it cool and discouraging bugs from invading the flour.

Cotton was picked by hand, stuffed in a Croker sack that was dragged along by each picker as they moved between the rows. The cotton had to be ginned to remove the seeds from the fiber. There was a home gin, a heavy metal box, a crank on the side and a cylinder with sharp spikes on the sides within the box. The cotton was fed through the top and the turning crank would pull and separate the seeds from the cotton fibers.

The ears of corn were broken in the fields when they had ripened. If the corn was ready to be pulled the tassels on the end would be dark brown. It was time to harvest before the kernels got too hard. The outside leaves were stripped from the cobs. There was a cast iron gizmo attached to a table where dried corn cobs were fed though, separating the corn kernels from the cobs, the empty cobs would fall into a basket and the corn kernels into another. For canning, the freshly picked corn, with silks removed, would be put in a large pot of water and heated until the water just started to boil. After the blanched cobs were completely cooled the ripe kernels could be sliced off by a sharp knife, then the corn could be canned for winter or cooked for their supper. In the fall the dried leaves were pulled from the corn stalks, bundled for fodder, and stored in the barn loft to feed the animals in the harsh cold of Winter.

* * * * *

One other child would be born to Uly and Martha, his name was Elijah Serenus Gantt. They just called him "Babe".

After Uly returned from the War in 1865, the family started to take the Sabbath more seriously. Uly had seen so many horrors in the War; rotting bodies left on the battle-field and stacks of arms and legs amputated, piled outside the surgeons' tent. These were awful memories, and he was looking for peace. It wasn't that he didn't practice his religion, grace was always said before a meal and the children said their nightly prayers supervised by their mother. Uly was always taught by his mother Lizzie about how important his belief in a higher power was and that all the children were taught to honor the Sabbath as a day of rest and to read the Bible. His Momma, Lizzie always did, and she taught her children to revere God's Word, but with the War he had fought in and the hard life they all lived, it was easy to lose sight of what is most important in life.

They, as a family, began to attend Convent Baptist Church. It was an old church, even when Uly and Martha's children were born. The church was founded in 1828, few attended during the War, too fearful, perhaps, but now Uly and Martha decided to start attending church again regularly. They wanted their children to be brought up as God fearing men and women. That was their goal and a good decision. Not only going to church on Sunday would feed the spirit, but way down Little Black Creek, they didn't do a lot of socializing, they were too busy living, working to survive. Attending church would mean they would make friends and communicate with others including a lot of relatives. So, every Sunday, Uly would hook up the mules to their old farm wagon, load up the kids and go to Convent to hear a good sermon and visit with friends and neighbors. Once a month after Sunday church they would have dinner on the grounds. Martha would cook some vegetables, a pie or cake and bring a gallon of sweet tea. Behind the church, under a big Oak tree, wooden tables shaded by a tin roof sat ready to hold all the great foods the church ladies brought. They would sit on the benches and eat their fill. While the ladies packed up their dishes and the leftovers, the menfolk would stand around discussing their crops, politics, or someone's misbehavior. They would chew their tobacco or smoke their cigars and freely offer their opinions on everything.

Convent Church is where Ella Jane met her future husband, Jerome Lucas. They married about 1890 and had ten children:

Ella Jane Gantt Lucas was born the 2nd of March 1866 died 17th of May 1955. Contrary to what her tombstone says, I believe she was born in the year 1866. Her father,

Uly, didn't get home from the War until June 1865 and nowhere on his War record does it state he had a furlough. I do not believe his wife, Martha, way down on Black Creek with four young children had a dalliance with someone beside her husband, Uly. Jerome Lucas was born the 11th of March 1869 and died 27th of August 1938.

Their Children were:

1. Elmer Elijah Lucas born 13th of November 1891 died 30th April 1960 married Sallie Marie Gantt
2. Annis Martha Lucas born 1892 died 1979 married Leighton Elvin Corbett
3. Fulton Andrew Lucas born 1894 died 1932 married Maude Rawls
4. Addie Jane Lucas born 1 August 1896 died 19th of January 1993 married 1st Andrew Govan Stevenson 1884-1956 2nd James William Spence 1882-1961. I knew Miss Addie well, she attended a few of our Gantt Reunions and I have a letter she sent to me per the request of her son, Floyd Davidson Spence Sr. Floyd was a U.S. Congressman, spending 30 years in that office. He was a Korean War Veteran and served more than 40 years in the Navy reserve, retiring at the rank of Captain.
5. Lawton Furman Lucas born 1898 died 1945 married Mary Gladys Rawls
6. Ila Mae Lucas born 1899 died 1992 married Alton Elbert Hall
7. Dantzler Charlie Lucas born 1901 died 1936 married Ottalee Lawson O'Toole

8. Earl Lucas born 1904 died 1965 married Barnette Dehart
9. Lever "Slim" Lucas born 1906 died 1969.
10. Lois Lucas born 1911 died 2001 married Herbert Sidney Beach

"The love between a mother and
daughter is FOREVER."

Ella Gantt Lucas, daughter of Elijah with her daughter Addie Lucas Spence and grandson Floyd Spence holding one of his sons.

20. The Second Daughter, Corrie

The second daughter of Uly and Martha was Corrie Martha Gantt, I have seen her name spelled both Carrie and Corrie, doesn't really matter. Her birth year is also a question. On her tombstone it is listed as 1872, but in all my research, the youngest and last child was Uncle Babe Gantt, he was born 1869, so in this story I am using 1867 as Aunt Corrie's birth year.

I have a letter I received from R. Cecil Fallaw, grandson of Corrie, in 1984. He talks about his grandmother and describes her life much better than I could and he knew her personally, so I will be quoting from Cecil's letter. I met Cecil personally at one of our early Gantt Reunions.

"You wrote to my mother for some information on my Grandmother last December and I did not realize she had not written back to you until today. She has been through quite a lot this past year and was not able to get this information for you. My father, who was the youngest child of Corrie Gantt Fallaw died a year ago (John F Fallaw born

1901 died 1983 from newspaper obituary) this past May, so my mother has had to get herself adjusted to a whole new lifestyle since that time — It has not been easy for any of us.

I don't have all the information you need at this time, but I have some and will get the rest for you in due time. I don't know now just when my Grandmother was born, but I think I can find out for you. She died March 21, 1951, and is buried in Cresent Hill Memorial Park on Two Notch road in Columbia, SC. She is buried there with her first son George Edison Gantt and her last, or second, Husband George Strickland. She first married a man we only know as V. Fallaw. He probably came from near Batesburg or Leesville and their marriage probably took place near the end of the nineteenth century. I don't know when, but I may be able to find out later for you. Her first child was probably born out of wedlock, no one ever talked about it. I don't know when or where he was born, but I would guess someplace between Pelion, SC, and Leesville SC in the late 1800's. I can find out later when he died, I think. I can only remember that he lived only a short time after his mother died, they were pretty close to each other and lived together the last part of their lives in the house with her Husband George Strickland.

Her second child was John Drayfus Fallaw. He was born May 10, 1900, near Fairview between Pelion & Leesville. He died in April 1970, don't know the date but can find out later. My father, John Feaster Fallaw, was born October 31, 1902, in the same area. He died May 29, 1983. Both Uncle Drayfus and my father are buried between

West Columbia and Lexington not too far apart. My father is in Celestial Memorial Garden and Uncle Drayfus is in Gibson Cemetery which is just across the road (Uncle Drayfus has marker in Gibson Cemetery, but it states Draifus W. Fallaw born May 1899 died Apr 1969 More confusion!). I think I remember my father saying he would have had a sister if she had not died, that's all I know about that. Also, I know very little about my Grandfather V. Fallaw. My Grandmother and V Fallaw left SC and moved to someplace in Florida when my Father was very young. She left her husband and came back to SC when my father was only 3 or 4 years old. He hardly knew his father at all. She came back here and raised her 3 sons alone. It was hard, they had very little of any material things, the boys didn't get much education, having to go to work in the textile mills when they were very young, probably 10 or 12 years old. My Father worked there until he was 62 and retired. He was 81 when he died. He lived longer than any of them.

The first son Edison Gantt had one son, where and when I don't know, who he is, I don't know. If he was married when this son was born, I don't even know this. He was married to Ruth Mcvey for a time, but no children came from this marriage.

The second son Drayfus Fallaw married Lillian Earheart they had 2 children, First Bertha Lee Fallaw born the early part of 1924. She is a few months older than me. Their second child was a boy, John Drayfus Fallaw Jr. born in 1925 or 1926. He lives in West Columbia now. Bertha Lee lives in the State of Washington on the west coast (Bertha Lee & John D Jr would be 1st cousins to Cecil who wrote this letter, you would think he would know, but more confusion).

The third son of Corrie Gantt, my father married Mollie L. Logan in 1923, she came from near Manning, SC. They had two sons, I was the first child, Ralph Cecil Fallaw born in what was New Brookland, SC later changed to West Columbia, SC. I was born July 5, 1924. My brother, Charlie David Fallaw was born March 6, 1927. He died in 1971 and is buried with my Father. Charlie was hit by an automobile in 1943 and lived the rest of his life in a wheelchair. He died of a heart attack.

I hope this information has helped you some. Also hope you can read it. You asked about a picture of my Grandmother. I will have to have a print made for you. Unfortunately, there is only one picture that I know of. My mother has that one. I was supposed to get some of Grandmother's personal things. But she died before her husband George Strickland, and he and his people got what little she had left. She married George Strickland in about 1934 or 35 and lived with him until she died.

Her brother, Jefferson Davis Gantt died in my father's house in West Columbia. I have tried to find out when. He was buried by Thompson Funeral Home West Columbia. I have asked them to look up their records but have not heard from them. I would guess he died in the thirties, 1935 or 1936. But unfortunately, I have no records at this time. He was married to Nancy Garrick from Columbia, I think. They had no children.

If I can help you in any other way, please write and let me know. My Grandmother was a fine little woman. She never had much but she didn't seem to expect too much. I loved her dearly."

Sincerely, R. Cecil Fallaw

To my readers, would you not agree, Aunt Corrie and her children led a sad life!

Corrie Martha Gantt, daughter of Uly and Martha born the 10th of September 1867 died 21st of March 1951 married 1st V. Fallaw 2nd George Strickland:

1. George Edison Gantt born 1892 died 18th of February 1952 (probably born out of wedlock.
2. Dreyfus W. Fallaw (the letter has his name as John Dreyfus) born 10th May 1900 died 16th April 1970
3. John Feaster Fallaw born 31st October 1901 died 29th May 1983

My Uncle spoke of Edison Gantt. He said Edison worked in the Mill in Columbia, the one that now is the SC State Museum, I believe it was called the Columbia Mill. Uncle Leon said Edison was a heavy drinker and frequently went to work drunk. But he also said Edison could spin and weave more cloth drunk than most of the other workers could sober. That's why the bosses never complained when Edison came in inebriated. His two brothers, Dreyfus and Feaster probably worked in the same cotton mill.

"You just can't beat the person who never gives up"

—Babe Ruth

Corrie M. Gantt Fallaw, daughter of Uly

R. Cecil Fallaw and wife, Helen Hook.

Feaster and Drayfus Fallaw, sons of Corrie Gantt Fallaw.

21. The Baby Boy of Uly and Martha: Elijah Serenus

Elijah Sereus Gantt "Babe" was born in the winter of 1869, February 23rd to be exact. It had been extremely cold since late November and the cold weather did not let up. The ground was heavy with frost and ice spewed up on the edge of Little Black Creek, where the water was calm. Martha was of course concerned about her baby boy and his survival due to the harsh weather. When she was able to return to her duties, she carried Babe in a sling close to her body to assure he stayed warm, swaddling him in a cozy blanket before placing him in the sling. Martha would carry Babe this way for the first month of his life. Afterwards, Martha kept him on a pallet in the kitchen house near the fire, so he was always within her eyesight.

As Babe grew, it became apparent he was full of personality. He smiled and cooed when any of his siblings talked to him, his laughter soon filled their home. He was such a happy baby and just being in his presence lifted the whole family's spirits. He soon became the trickster in the family and when he learned to talk, he never shut up. After Crummy sent him sailing through the open beams of the kitchen house, at age three, Babe was always trying to play little tricks on the other members of the family, his siblings anyway. Martha and Uly would not take kindly to his little jokes. Babe became the constant entertainer in the family. The gun powder ride through the rafters Crummy sent him on would always be a fond memory. After a time, it became one of his favorite stories.

He realized when he was older that Crummy was right, he was a stubborn little shit, and he was never mad with Crummy. He still chuckled when he thought of the ingenuity of his older brother. He was very close to Crummy and knew Crummy was a good father, taking care of their children after Priscilla, his wife, had died at age 42, leaving Crummy to be both mother and father to their brood. He really admired his brother. They spent lots of time together, hunting, fishing, and exploring the land where they were born. Of course, like their brothers, they helped Uly, pushing plows and taking care of their livestock.

Babe grew up in the family home on Little Black Creek and would remain in the Black Creek area all his life. He and brother, Crummy, would raise their families in the shadow of the others, above Big Black Creek and Uly's pond.

Babe had two sons, Woodrow and Daniel. Woodrow always had his father's personality. He was a big talker too. As a child, I witnessed Woodrow's knack for conversation. I went to Gantt's Store on highway 178, halfway between Fairview and Pelion quite often. I visited there even as a teenager, on return trips from basketball games. The general store, as these small communities called them, had a variety of products that all families needed, saving them from a much longer trip to a town.

Every little community had a general store, it seems in the 1920's until the 1950's and 1960's. There was Mr. Cleve Padgett's store in Fairview, Mr. Cliff Rish's in Steedman, and of course Gantt's near Black Creek. I remember going to these stores in my childhood. I have to say, Gantt's was by far the best. If they didn't have what you requested, you didn't need it. The shelves and the walls were covered with products from farm implements, canned foods, fresh produce, tools, automotive parts, and everything in between.

My Uncle, Roston Gantt, ran a general store in Rayflin much earlier and had his products shipped by the train to stock the store. That would be the "Swamp Rabbit", part of the Mid Carolina Railroad. It connected Batesburg and Perry, SC. I have a copy of the legal document that my Great Grandparents, Jacob Kelly and Peninnah Gantt signed agreeing to give the Carolina Midlands railroad right of way. It was to extend fifty feet from the center of the track, cost to Carolina Midlands was five dollars, signed the 7th day of August 1891. The track was actually constructed in 1898 and was actively used until 1933.

As a child, I can remember a huge deep gully behind our old house and between there and the North Edisto River. There were many pieces of broken railroad ties dumped into this gully, maybe when the "Swamp Rabbit" was built? We played there sixty-five years ago. That memory just returned, a surprise. I haven't thought of that in over fifty years.

Gantt's store was actually built in the 1920's by Uncle Babe, with help from his brothers. Uncle Babe's two sons, his boys Daniel, the bookkeeper, and Woodrow, the talker, helped their father run the general store and did so until the late 1970's when age caught up with them. Uncle Babe himself probably spent many evenings with his boys and customers at the store. It was a central meeting place for locals, good conversation, laughter, and music from a radio perched on the shelf behind Daniel and the counter that held his adding machine.

There was a lot of activity during the Depression when moonshiners were active in the community. My Grandaddy, Kelly Gantt, was a first cousin of Daniel and Woodrow. Kelly and his son Leon, my uncle, were big moonshiners in the 1930's. Uncle Babe's brother, Jacob Kelly "Kell" passed away in 1930 and for the next seven years a number of liquor stills were run on Kell's property, near the North Edisto River. As long as Kell was alive and able, he would not allow his sons to run moonshine stills.

Great Grandpa Kell was not a teetotaler, but he did not hold with breaking the law. If he found a still on his land, he would bust it up. I say this as prelude to a moonshine story my Uncle Leon told me that took place in Gantt's store with Woodrow as a main actor. My other books have lots of moonshine stories, but actually I do not believe I have recorded this story.

From Leon Gantt, his story: "When I was deep into the moonshine business, I was with some of my friends at

Gantt's store. The radio was playing, this was probably early 1930's after my Granddaddy Kell had passed away. He wouldn't let a still remain on his land if he knew about it. I say 1930's because that is when I made most of my liquor. The last two years I was making liquor, I was drunk the whole time. I basically lost two years of my life. I quit cold turkey on the 1st of July 1937.

"Me and a bunch of my usual drinking buddies were out at the store late one Saturday night, just me and a bunch of old drunks. Woodrow had a few himself. Asia Gunter was there, he was a queer man, but entertaining and we never held that against him. Asia was drinking pretty heavy too. There was some good country music on Daniel's radio, Kitty Wells, Tex Ritter, The Carter family and Roy Acuff, old music stars that could really sing. Asia decided he wanted to dance. Him and Woodrow started sashaying around in front of that wood stove that sat in the middle of the store.

"When Woodrow said, 'Asia if we're going to dance, you need a dress on.'

"Asia replied, 'Well Woodrow, where in the hell am I going to get a dress?' 'We'll make you one,' said Woodrow.

"On the floor sat a Croker sack full of cabbages. I said, 'Asia, let's make you a dress out of this Croker sack, so I dumped the damn cabbage in a cardboard box on the floor and took out my knife and proceeded to cut a large hole in the bottom big enough to go over Asia's head and a hole on either side for his arms. Asia took off his outer shirt and I helped him get that Croker sack over his head and his arms through the sides.

"While Asia was putting on the dress, Woodrow lit a

big stogy, must have been six or eight inches long. Well, Woodrow started puffing on his cigar and him and Asia commenced to dancing. I could see, right away, this was not going to work. Woodrow blowing smoke into Asia's eyes and jabbing him with the burning cigar. They were both pretty well drunk at this time.

"Asia stopped suddenly and stepped back from his partner and said earnestly, 'Woodrow, I'm enjoying this dancing right much, but you're going to have to get shed of that Cigar!'

"The whole bunch of us, almost fell on the floor laughing at Asia, he just remained quiet. He finally said earnestly, 'I don't understand why you boys think that's so funny.'

Elijah Serenus "Babe" Gantt, born the 23rd of February 1869, died the 15th of August 1955. Uncle Babe married Nancy Elizabeth McCartha, born the 16th of February 1876, died the 4th of September 1949. They had four children:

1. Daniel Franklin Gantt, born the 10th of November 1906, died the 6th of June 1992, married Kitty Peale, no children. Daniel served as Tech 5 in the U.S. Army in WWII.
2. Ellen Gantt, born 14th of May 1908, died 21st of November 2001, married Marion Edward Williams, born 13th of December 1911, died 10th of October 1965.
3. Jesse Woodrow Gantt, born 7th of June 1911, died 26th of October 1995, married to Juanita Fallaw Gantt. Inscription on Woodrow's tombstone, A

Father, Store Owner, Whittler, "Talker", and Animal Lover.

4. Emmie Marie Gantt Zook, born 30 of April 1914, died 12 March 1999, married Sherman Paul Zook 1904-1953.

"Treat your family like friends and
your friends like family."

Elijah Serenus 'Babe' Gantt, son of Uly

Woodrow Gantt, son of Babe Gantt, grandson of Uly and Martha.

22. "Chickens Come Home to Roost"

"Neither snow nor rain nor heat nor gloom of night" … nor Secession will stop the delivery of the mail. A Mr. Joe Campbell delivered the mail riding in a covered carriage pulled by a strong grey mule. Mr. Joe was simply addressed as the mail man. He didn't visit Martha often when Uly was away in the War, but after the War, mail picked up. With no other means of keeping in touch, people would send a simple postcard to their kin folks just to let them know any news and that they were "still above the grass", living and breathing. If their kin lived further along on Mr. Campbell's route, the postcard was usually delivered the same day.

A touch of winter was already in the air that October of 1877, Martha and her girls, Ella and Corrie were busy in the kitchen house. They had put up a big barrel of collard kraut. Chopped collards, approximately a cup of salt and enough water to cover the collards with the salty brine was the recipe passed down for generations. A clean towel was secured in place to keep the kraut completely covered. The chopped collards would be left to ferment for at least five days, then it could be stored in jars in a cool place. The kraut barrel now sat against the kitchen house wall.

A chilly breeze blew over the creek the day the mailman appeared at Uly and Martha's home. It was a bumpy ride down the old wagon road. No matter, Mr. Campbell was a dedicated employee and used to sand beds and bumpy roads. The younger boys, Davis, Crummy, and Babe were out in the fields with Uly bundling the dried corn leaves and cutting the stalks with a stalk-cutter. The dried leaves, fodder, would help feed their livestock come cold weather.

On this October morning, Mailman Campbell left an official looking letter addressed to Ulysess Gantt from the tax office located in the Lexington County Courthouse. Curiosity got the better of Martha and she opened the letter. It was a statement of back taxes since 1860 for 2,200 acres of land. Martha immediately realized what acreage the bill referred to, her inheritance.

In Chapter 13 of my story, the fact was brought out that Uly Gantt and his brother-in-law, Cary Rawls mortgaged two thousand two hundred acres of land to James D. Jones on the bank of Big Black Creek. The War started soon thereafter in 1861 and the interest and the payment that was supposed to be paid to Mr. Jones was not paid. This mortgage was not revealed to Martha Matilda and her sister, Amanda, who married Cary Rawls. Well, like most sneaky moves, Martha found out and she was absolutely livid that her husband would stoop so low as to mortgage her land inheritance without her knowledge. She only found out when that back tax bill arrived in the fall of 1877. How would she have known, Uly was still planting the acreage and she had no sign that it did not belong to the family legally. But that was about to change.

When Martha finished reading the delinquent tax notice, she was absolutely livid that she was not consulted. She had to sit down, try to stay calm, and think about what was the best course of action. How should she proceed? She didn't want to upset any of the children by having a shouting match with Uly in their presence. She knew that would accomplish nothing. Deciding she had to consult someone she trusted, she thought of her eldest son, Kell. He was already married to Penninah Woodward and lived at Rayflin on the North Edisto River. She would send a postcard to her eldest son, Jacob Kelly 'Kell" Gantt asking him to come and see her as soon as possible about a private matter. She also said, "We're all fine, just need you to stop by."

She couldn't express her feelings honestly on a postcard that could be read by anyone whose hands it passed through. She liked the mailman, Mr. Campbell, but she didn't even trust him to be quiet. He would take it the next day. She decided she would try to keep her feelings to herself until she could confide in Kell. She stuffed the letter back into the envelope, folding it, she put it in her apron pocket away from prying eyes. She would hide the delinquent tax notice in the Bible until she could confer with Kell.

A few days later, Kell came to check on his mother, they took a buggy ride and stopped a little way from the house by the creek to have a private conversation. She told Kell of the discovery and handed him the tax bill. After Martha's explanation and reading the letter, Kell, said, "Ma you and I will go to the courthouse in Lexington and talk to the Clerk of Court, Mr. Asseman. We'll explain the deception by Pa, I'm sure he'll give us the right advice and it will be according to the law."

Kell and Martha did have a meeting with Mr. Assman. The result, Martha filed a bill of complaint on the 23rd of October in 1877. The complaint was filed against her husband Uly Gantt and Cary Rawls.

I was told there was some problem with Martha and Uly's relationship in 1995 and that she threw him out of the house, so for almost 120 years there were people that still were aware of the break in their relationship and were willing to talk about it. Sometimes gossip never dies.

The case of Martha's complaint against Uly and Cary was heard in Lexington County by William J Asseman, Clerk of Common Pleas. The case was heard on the 15th of June 1881. Just like in today's world, the wheels of justice turn slowly. In the meantime, Uly, had to find himself another abode, not with his wife, Martha. She, with Kell, did confront him and told him what he had to do. He did appear contrite and sorry for the mess he and Cary had caused and swore he would make it right. He really loved Martha. Uly did move out, he pretty much became a vagabond like his son Davis, staying a couple months at a time with each of his children. So much had happened since he and Cary originally mortgaged that property, the War, and hard times for everybody, even Mr. James D. Jones who had given Uly and Cary the money for the land, had lost everything. He couldn't afford to pay the back taxes and reclaim the property.

The case was heard on the 15th day of June 1881. The Court decided "the land here in after mentioned should be sold at public auction by the Clerk of Court." The public auction did take place at the Lexington Courthouse. Martha was represented by her son, Kell, and the land was sold at auction to Mrs. Martha M. Gantt for the sum of fifteen hundred and seventy-five dollars. The land was described as containing 2,200 acres more or less on Black Creek waters of the North Edisto River, dated the 7th of November 1881. The deed was delivered November the 24th 1882. After reviewing a complicated legal document, Martha M. Gantt signed the 14th day of August 1884. The land was now legally in her hands.

Beginning in 1891, Martha began to parcel out her property to her children. The land records of Lexington County show Martha M. Gantt transferring land to her children for one dollar and love and affection. Kell was her trustee and responsible for upholding her wishes as to the land division. An entry of the 12th of March 1894 shows that Ulysses "Uly" Gantt gave to his wife Martha M. Gantt 2,000 dollars paid through her trustee, Kell Gantt. His conscience got the best of him, and he repaid Martha the money he owed.

I was told by my uncle, Leon, that Uly and Martha made up before his death and that they were living togeth er again. Uly passed away the 22nd of September 1897. It appears they lived as husband and wife for the last three years before his death. Martha is buried beside Uly at John Gunter Mill cemetery near Seivern, SC. Martha died the 23rd of October 1913, her eldest son Kell, is still mentioned as her trustee. I do know from the settlement of her estate that it was worth only 1,000 dollars, those who signed the final settlement were: Kell (J.K Gantt), E.S. Gantt (Babe), and T.R. Gantt (the eldest son of Kell, Thomas Roston).

Martha M. spent the last years of her life living with Uncle Crummy Gantt and his family. I have a picture that verifies that, a picture of Crummy, wife Annie Priscilla Lucas. Crummy's mother, Martha Matilda Cook Gantt is standing in the center of the family picture. Cilla (Crummy's wife) is in this picture holding a small child, she passed away in 1909. Leading to the conclusion that Martha was living with Crummy at her death in 1913.

"Marriage isn't about Winning. It's about Lasting."

—Mark Gorman

Tombstone of Ulysses 'Uly' Gantt, John Gunter Mill Cemetery, Seivern SC.

Tombstone of Martha Matilda Cook Gantt, wife of Uly.

Cary and Amanda Cook Rawls.

Epilogue: Irreplaceable Memories

There were several traits I began to notice as I put all my research on the Gantt Family together by generations, I hope in the correct order. Characteristics and traits that show up in almost every generation. I noted earlier in my compilation of research that the same Christian names were passed on over and over again to other generations, making it extremely difficult to keep the genealogical lines separate. Most of the twelve generations included in this book, before my own, are names found in the Bible, names like Elijah, Eli, Samuel, James, John, Zebulon, etc. on the paternal side, names like Martha, Mary, Hannah, Elizabeth, and even Tirzah for the maternal.

One other trait that stands out to me after writing most of the Gantt story would be their work ethic and the occupations they followed to sustain their families. There were many that farmed their land, "By the sweat of your brow you will have food to eat until you return to the ground, from which you were made." (Genesis 3:19 Holy Bible NLT)

The above verse makes it clear biblically that it will take hard work to earn your food. The earlier generations were mostly farmers, tanners, carpenters, and photographers in the Gantt families. In the early twentieth century, turpentine distillers and of course production of moonshine was a popular business, the production of moonshine was illegal so would not have been broadcast as an occupation. These trades and names are what compose the roots of the Gantt family tree and the branches that spread from the trunk and into the future.

Surnames are intermingled with each other, especially in the 19th century. It is always a dilemma when doing research in that time period and region. It was Gantt, Gunter, Rish, Padgett, Shumpert, Miller, Quattlebaum, Shealy, and Hall. These surnames show up in every generation and always in the Lexington, Aiken, and Orangeburg Districts. If you are researching a family with any of these surnames, it is likely their original ancestors are from one of these districts in South Carolina. It creates a nightmare for genealogists when trying to correctly separate the family lines. They also married someone, in many cases, with one of these surnames too. It gets more confusion when this occurs. Case in point, my stepmother was a Gantt, married a Gunter, then married a Gantt, my father, Robert. Her mother was a Gunter married Gantt; it gets more confusing as we research further back. I did my best and hope I kept everyone in the right generation. Of course, when you think about it, travel was not easy back then. Most people ended up marrying close neighbors, which in turn, means they were quite possibly related.

The Gantts of Aiken and Lexington Districts were, with few exceptions, honest, patriotic, and hard-working people. The one exception to rule in that time period would be the notorious outlaw, Emmanuel Williams, his mother was a Gantt. I wrote this book to tell their story. It is a fictional account of their lives, historically the names, places, and dates are actually true. All the characters are real except for the Browns who were servants of Joseph Gauntt from Newberry and the name of the mailman, Mr. Campbell in the last chapter I wrote _Legacy, In search of the Past_ to honor all of my Gantt ancestors and to leave a story of their lives, a narrative. It makes it more interesting to the reader and is actually based on the lives that people lived in that time and place, not just names and dates.

It was not really hard to make their stories sound believable because my childhood was so much like my 19th century counterparts. We were not well off, there was much farming and raising livestock before I was born in 1951. My Daddy worked in a cotton mill, it was not a lavish lifestyle, but it was wonderful. I heard these kinds of stories every day in my childhood and beyond. We went to school on a school bus, returned the same way. In the winter, it would be late when we got home, evening was beginning to settle around the old house, the sun low behind the tall junipers in the west. We still had to fill up the wood boxes on both porches to insure the house was moderately warm, especially the kitchen, where homework was done, and the television stood. With only three channels, we didn't care what program was on, we would watch.

There were no security lights outside, just darkness and

lots of stories told on the front porch by Uncle Leon, my Daddy, Robert, and my Grandma's brothers. My Grandma, Florence, pretty much raised us four kids and she was born in 1887. You can imagine, we thought she was ancient.

I still lay awake almost every night, just thinking and remembering. Before sleep engulfs me like a cozy blanket and I surrender my mind to dreams, the memories of my childhood, consume my thoughts. It is like time travel to the 1950's, and I remember. Those nights sitting quietly on the front porch listening to the murmuring voices of my elders talking and telling stories about who lived where, how their farms were tended or not, and what the sermon was about last Sunday and whether they agreed with the theme of the sermon or not.

I remember visiting relatives at night, traveling over sandy roads, no street signs or light, except the car lights. I can remember the mounds of dirt that marked the side of those empty, dark roads, looking out the car windows and seeing the roadside with broom straw on top of the mounds near the road. Sunday was the day to visit our relatives and friends. The rest of the week was for work. We would have company on Sundays only in my childhood, unless it was near relatives that visited in the evening to sit on the porch, smoke, chew, and discuss topics of interest that affected their lives and ours.

My favorite memories are sitting on that front porch, no light except a blanket of stars above and the bright yellow moon as it rose above the horizon. Once I remember a squirrel jumping from tree to tree, I was told it was a flying squirrel with flaps of skin between the front and back legs, it didn't actually jump from tree to tree, it glided. The only one I remember seeing. The night sounds I remember most were crickets, whippoorwills, hoot owls, and sometimes barking dogs in the distance.

The sights were the stars in heaven and the lightening bugs across the road flashing their little taillights in the dark woods. Depending on the season, the smells could be Grandma's flowers, honeysuckle in the woods nearby, Grandma's cooking, drifting out through the screen door and of course the porch sitters smoking cigars and cigarettes. It was a wonderful childhood, and I am thankful, God gave me that childhood. I miss that dark front porch, the stories from the old folks, and the night sounds. Sometimes I wish I could go back!

Sources Cited

Books:

Butler, Dennis. *1066, The Story of a Year*: G.P. Putnam's Sons, 1966

Douglas, David C. *William The Conqueror*. Berkeley & Los Angles: University of California Press, 1964.

Mac, Gerard. *Pilgrims—A Novel About the Mayflower*. St. Martin's Press, 1994.

Woodward, William E. *The Way Our People Lived*: Washington Square Press, New York, 1965.

Chapman, John A. *Annals of Newberry*. Aull & Houseal, 1892, 461.

Blackman, Leah. *History of Little Egg Harbor*. Reprinted by the Higginson Book Company, Salem MA, originally printed 1880. 285-294.

Woolman, John. *The Journal of John Woolman and a Plea for the Poor*. The Citadel Press. Secaucus N.J. 5th paper bound printing. 1961.

Mortimer, Ian. *The Time Travelers Guide to Elizabethan England*: Penguin Books. 1967.

Gauntt, David. *Peter Gaunt 1610-1680 and some of his descendants*. Gloucester County Historical Society. Woodbury, N.J. 1989.

Bryan, Gus J. and Ruby R. *Covington County History 1821-1976*. Covington Publishing Company. Opp Alabama, 1976, 251-256.

Hilborn, Nat & Sam. *Battleground of Freedom, South Carolina In The Revolution*. Sandlapper Press Inc., Columbia S.C.

Pamphlets and Magazine:

Peter Gaunt of Massachusetts and his Descendants. Compiled and written by Connie Jo Geary. Annandale Va. January 1981.

Harmon, Daniel. *The Bloody Legacy of Emmanuel Williams*. Published in Saxe-Gotha. August 1980.

Setton, Kenneth M. "The Norman Conquest". *The National Geographic*. 130.2 (1966) 206-251.

Interviews:

Stories of Leon O. Gantt 1910-2001, my Uncle

Frank Joseph Gantt 1907-1989, my Step Grandfather

Robert Kelly Gantt 1923-2015, my Father

Digital interview of Dr. Aubrey Gantt 1924-2009, Grandson of Luther

Luther Lafayette 1858-1932

www.ingramcontent.com/pod-product-compliance
Lightning Source LLC
Chambersburg PA
CBHW022122310726
48972CB00007B/2149